"I NEED YOU, PENELOPE. SAY YOU WILL MARRY ME."

Penelope could not find the breath to answer. All she had ever wanted, from the first moment she had seen him, was now hers with a mere nod of the head. The wonderment of her dearest wish come true astonished her beyond words.

Before she could reply, he kissed her. He was still smiling down upon her when his eyes lit up with mischief. "I have severely compromised your honor. It behooves me to make an honest woman of you." He reached out to stroke her hair. "You must marry me now, do you know that?"

Penelope pulled back from him, her face frozen in stunned disbelief.

"This was a trap!" she accused.

❄

Suddenly
A Lady

Melinda Pryce

DIAMOND BOOKS, NEW YORK

This book is a Diamond original edition, and has never
been previously published.

SUDDENLY A LADY

A Diamond Book/published by arrangement with
the author

PRINTING HISTORY
Diamond edition/July 1992

ISBN: 1-55773-741-X

Diamond Books are published by The Berkley Publishing Group,
200 Madison Avenue, New York, New York 10016.
The name "DIAMOND" and its logo are trademarks
belonging to Charter Communications, Inc.

PRINTED IN THE UNITED STATES OF AMERICA

10 9 8 7 6 5 4 3 2 1

To my Critique Group,
who stuck by the gravedigger's
daughter until she was
suddenly a lady.

Suddenly
A Lady

CHAPTER
ONE

PENELOPE GRAVES WAS hopelessly lost.

"Take this to the ladies and gentlemen in the library," she repeated the butler's orders aloud. She shook her head with exasperation. "I only work here as kitchen help. How should I know where the library is?"

She shifted the weight of the large silver tray. She had believed the tray manageable enough when she first took it up, but it rapidly grew heavier as she searched the seemingly interminable corridors of Bellford Manor for her intended destination.

"How do those lords and ladies succeed in finding their way about each other's houses? I've never heard of any of *them* becoming lost," she muttered to herself. Then she grinned as she thought, 'Still, I suppose I should be grateful old Lord Bellingsford has a nice, clean mansion instead of some moldy old castle with dank, rat-infested dungeons for me to lose myself in.'

Penelope espied a solitary gentleman farther down the corridor. He stood with his back to her, studying one of the numerous paintings that adorned the walls. She knew it would be considered rude for a mere servant such as she to impose upon one of Lord Bellingsford's houseguests. Still, it could do no harm merely to ask the gentleman for something as simple as assisting her with directions.

"Excuse me, sir," she said hesitantly.

"Are you speaking to me?" the gentleman asked. As he turned slowly about, his eyes met hers.

1

She drew in a sharp breath to accommodate her heart as it leaped and pounded against her chest.

Four years had passed since she had last seen Corbett Remington. Four years—certainly time enough in which to believe oneself completely recovered from a broken heart. Now she knew that if she continued to stare at his squared chin and firm cheekbones, his deep blue eyes and the dark brows that arched above them, she stood in grave danger of becoming once again hopelessly lost to the pain of a love unreturned.

'Come now, Penelope,' she chided herself harshly. 'You're a woman of one and twenty, not some mawkish miss of seventeen. You cannot stand about with a tray in your hands all night. You have a duty to perform.' She drew in another deep breath as if she could draw in additional courage as well. 'And you *mustn't* allow the man ever to know how he hurt you!' She knew she would need every ounce of fortitude she could muster if she were to succeed in that.

She swallowed hard to hide the choking sensation that arose in her throat. "I am having difficulty in finding the library, sir. Could you please direct me to . . .?"

"One would suppose the help to be properly oriented before turning them loose in the house," Corbett said with a small shake of his head.

He had called her merely "the help," Penelope noted sadly. 'Well, why should he remember me?' she asked herself.

"I only serve here from time to time, sir," she attempted to explain. "That is why I—"

"Penelope!" he declared forcefully.

He *had* recognized her!

He made a sound which Penelope believed to be a chuckle, yet no smile curved his fine lips. "Did you think I would not remember you?" he chided her gently.

She nodded, then rapidly shook her head no.

"I thought perhaps you had not remembered *me*," he continued.

Not remember him? she silently cried. It certainly was not for lack of trying!

Corbett, the impoverished country squire's son, had come for his daily lessons to the vicarage where Penelope's mother served as the housekeeper. For years she had watched him, following him about with undisguised girlish adoration. He had seemed quite pleased to tolerate her devotion. He had not minded when the other fellows teased him about his little shadow. He had even come to her defense when their taunting occasionally turned nasty. For that, she had adored him all the more.

But when his father unexpectedly inherited a title from some distant, long-forgotten relation, Corbett bade the Reverend Mr. Wroxley a brief farewell and Penelope a cold adieu, then headed for what pleasures London could offer a young man. He was the heir apparent of the Viscount Ormsley, while she was only the daughter of the humble village sexton and far beneath his notice. Penelope determined then and there that if their paths should ever cross again, she would greet him as coldly as he had departed from her.

Why then, now, did her knees quiver and her hands clench tightly about the edge of the silver tray? Why did she want to drop this blasted tray and envelop him in a welcoming embrace? She thought she had quite recovered from his cold rejection. Yes, she told herself emphatically, she *had*. Therefore, she would do no such thing! But it disturbed her that she still wanted to hold him so badly.

"I am surprised to find you working here," Corbett said. "I supposed you to be married by now and caring for a home and family of your own."

Having once been hurt, Penelope had vowed never again to allow any man the opportunity to hurt her that way. How could she admit, even to herself, that the few men who had attempted to court the sexton's elusive daughter could never compare to Corbett Remington?

"I am not married, so I must work for a living," she told

him with a calmness that belied the quaking of her heart, quakings that reverberated to her very extremities.

"Yet you say you only serve here from time to time."

Penelope paused with surprise. Had he actually paid attention to what she said?

"I know Lord Bellingsford to be a generous man, yet I had not supposed him to be so magnanimous with his servants' wages that they need only work 'from time to time.' "

Again Penelope heard Corbett make the semblance of a chuckle. Still his face remained impassive. Wistfully, she recalled how his youthful laughter had animated his entire face. In gaining a title, she thought, had Corbett lost his smile?

"I usually help my mother at the vicarage as a maid-of-all-work," Penelope explained. "But of late I must assume more of her duties as housekeeper. I am afraid she becomes rather forgetful at times."

"I am sorry to hear that," Corbett said. From the tone of his voice, Penelope might believe that he truly was. "And your father?"

"He is well."

"I assume that means that his good nature allows him to tolerate the village boys' occasional pranks," Corbett inquired. "The tangled ropes?"

Penelope nodded.

"The frog in the milk pitcher?"

Penelope grimaced.

"Have they had the audacity to upset the Jericho again?"

Penelope grinned in spite of herself. "Not recently."

Corbett solemnly raised his right hand and pinioned her eyes with his steady gaze. "I never participated in any of that foolishness."

"I never thought you did," she replied softly.

More than anything, Penelope wanted to break away from the gaze that held her prisoner. She could not remain here, watching him, longing for something that she could never have. Yet more than anything, she wanted to stay, gazing into his deep blue eyes.

As she studied the unruly waves that caressed his high, broad forehead, she was seized with the same old bittersweet longing to reach out and smooth those waves back into their proper place. How often she had wanted to make that tender gesture—and yet she had never dared! Nor would she dare now. No doubt he would never allow her. Remembering his callous rejection gave her the strength to break his gaze.

"At any rate," she said, looking away, "the pranks were never dangerous, merely bothersome."

Corbett glanced down at the carpet. "How fares the good Reverend Mr. Wroxley?"

"His gout is a bit more troublesome. I suppose his age is beginning to tell on him as much as my mother's is on her."

Corbett nodded his understanding.

"I've only come to help in the kitchen tonight because of the ball." She indicated the heavy tray, which, while talking to Corbett, she had miraculously forgotten existed.

"Ah, yes. You were searching for the library, as I recall."

Penelope nodded, again surprised that Corbett should remember a mere fragment of their earlier conversation.

" 'Tis in this direction." Corbett extended his arm to indicate their destination.

Penelope felt his other hand barely touching her back as he prompted her to go on. With exceeding relief, she felt him move his hand away as suddenly as he had raised it. If the contact had lasted one second longer, she believed she surely would have dropped the tray.

There had been a time when she had dreamed of him, speculated about how his lips would feel upon hers, longed for his embrace. Yet, never had her dreams been realized. After Corbett left, she had done her utmost to forget her foolish desires. Now, one chance encounter had ruined everything.

'Now,' she thought forlornly, 'I shall have to start forgetting him all over again!'

Corbett led her a mere two doors farther down the long corridor.

'I could have found the library on my own if I had searched a bit longer,' Penelope thought with a small grimace, 'and never have had to encounter Corbett Remington again at all.' She released a tiny sigh. 'Never have had to remember how much he meant to me—and how little I meant to him. Never have had to remember how much I still hurt.'

Still, she thought as she glanced up at him from out of the corner of her eye, she was glad that she had seen him—just once more.

Corbett opened the door, then stepped back to allow Penelope, with her large, heavy tray, to pass.

"Thank you—" She stopped quickly. She had been upon the verge of calling him Corbett, for that was how she always thought of him. Yet now he was the Honorable Mr. Remington, and some day he would be Lord Ormsley. So she merely repeated more quietly, "Thank you."

Corbett regarded her intently. "So glad to have been of service," he said softly. "I wish you well, Penelope." He bowed, then turned away. He had been kind enough to assist her in finding her way. That would have to suffice. How foolish of her ever to hope he might linger with a mere serving maid.

She sadly watched him as he strode away, returning to *his* proper place at Lord Bellingsford's ball and leaving her to serve the tray and return to *her* proper place in Lord Bellingsford's kitchen.

With each step Corbett took down the empty corridor, he felt as if his feet were leaden weights. His heart lay like iron against his breastbone—and Penelope was the lodestone that pulled relentlessly at him.

He allowed a small smile of fond remembrance to spread briefly across his lips. Penelope's eyes were still the same unusual shade of soft, pale green. Her hair was still the same color of ripened wheat, although now, instead of allowing it to flow loosely about her shoulders, she wore it in a spinsterish knot wrapped tightly at the base of her slender neck.

He yearned to turn back to her, to enfold her in his arms and unfasten that beastly-looking knot, freeing her captive tresses. He longed to gaze into her pale green eyes and kiss her soft, full lips.

More than anything, he wanted to tell her how much he had missed her, how much he still loved her after all these years. How he had always loved her!

Then he quickly resumed his customary solemn expression. He continued to walk toward the gradually crescendo-ing strains of lilting music that echoed down the corridor from the ballroom. He had no time to waste on frivolous memories and foolish speculations about things that could never be. He had responsibilities, and a duty to perform. He *must* return to Lord Bellingsford's ball and all the lovely, eligible ladies dancing there.

Ormsley was a much-respected title, but what the previous viscount had managed to keep secret from everyone but his solicitor was the fact that there was precious little left of the once vast Ormsley wealth.

"You must marry an heiress—and soon," Peter Remington had commanded his son when their solicitor had informed them of this sorry fact upon his succession four years ago. " 'Tis your family duty to see that there is not only a continuation of the line, but an increase in its fortunes as well."

When Corbett hesitated, his father insisted. "You have no brothers to do it for you, son. After your mother died, I . . . I never had the heart to remarry."

Still Corbett hesitated to take such a drastic, and permanent, step. His father had inherited as a long-lost cousin. Upon Corbett's succession and eventual demise in the hopefully distant future, could not another long-lost cousin be found?

"It may seem a slight matter when you're a mere stripling of one and twenty," his father had scolded him for his frivilous reply, "but when a man has attained the ripe old age of five and forty, as have I, he begins to take more seriously the necessity for grandchildren."

Corbett had tried, truly he had. For the past four years, he had been dutifully bored at Almack's and every other stylish station along the Marriage Mart. No other lady, regardless of her accomplishments, connections, or fortune, had attracted him as had the young girl who had watched him with such adoration while he sat in the cozy vicarage study, poring over his books of geometry, Latin, and Greek.

Yet, for the sake of his family's title and estates, Corbett knew he could never wed Penelope—and for the sake of his own conscience, and her honor, he would never allow himself to have her any other way.

Carefully hidden from sight in the doorway, Penelope watched Corbett depart. The candlelight glinted in the dark brown hair that waved softly over the back of his head. She studied the smooth expanse of his broad shoulders that tapered to his long back and slim hips and muscular legs.

Never once had he looked back.

She pressed her lips tightly together. 'What a pity his father's succession to a title turned Corbett into a pompous ass,' Penelope thought. What an even greater pity to realize that she was still such a fool as to be in love with him!

With a deep sigh, she turned and entered the library.

"My gracious," she whispered aloud. She stared in awe as her eyes rose up the vast array of leather-bound volumes arranged against the walls. The Reverend Mr. Wroxley's study never looked anything like this! How wonderful it would be, the wistful thought ran through her mind, to be able to spend a lifetime in here.

Reluctant to break the silence of the shadowy library, she set the heavy tray on one of the many card tables that had been arranged about the room. But where were the ladies and gentlemen who intended to spend the evening here playing at cards?

"Why, little Penelope, isn't it?" came the slurred recognition.

Penelope started at the sound of the voice. She snapped her attention to the young gentleman who had just risen, rather unsteadily, from the large chair that had hidden him from her sight when she first entered.

He clumsily brushed a strand of fair hair back from his wide forehead. He blinked slowly, then drew his brows closer together over his bloodshot amber eyes and stretched his neck forward as if that would help him better to focus upon her. The brandy snifter cradled in both hands trembled noticeably.

'Bradley Fairmount, of all people!' Penelope silently lamented when she recognized Lord Bellingsford's nephew. 'Without a doubt, drunk again.' She suddenly felt a sense of mounting panic. 'Merciful heavens! And me here alone with him!'

Her eyes darted nervously to the corners of the room, as if the missing card players might suddenly, and most welcomely, materialize from thin air. Step by slow, careful step, Penelope made to retreat.

"Come back," Bradley called, waving her toward him with an awkward gesture of his hand. "No need to run from me. I'm completely harmless."

Penelope eyed him skeptically. Indeed, 'twas true that the worst gossip she had heard among the servants regarding Bradley Fairmount was that the young man had an inordinate passion for drinking and gambling. 'Twas his valet, the chambermaids whispered amongst themselves, who was to be avoided.

Most probably, Bradley was only here at Bellford Manor now because he had already squandered this quarter's allowance in London's gaming hells and was hiding out from the duns. What a great pity, Penelope thought, that kindly old Lord Bellingsford had no surviving offspring of his own and that this nephew was his heir.

Lord Bellingsford had remained unmarried after his wife was killed in a carriage accident twenty-one years ago. The body of the infant with her had never been recovered. Most of the villagers gruesomely maintained that the baby had been dragged off by wild dogs. A few of the more morbidly inclined had volunteered to search the woods for the tiny remains, but in spite of their zealous endeavors, no trace was ever found. As the coachman, footman, and nanny had also been killed, no one would ever know the true fate of the child.

Bradley tried to place the snifter on the small table beside his chair, but missed. The glass and its contents tumbled to the floor.

"Oh, dear," he said as he watched the dark, spreading stain ruin the lovely carpet. " 'Twould appear I've had just a tiny bit too much to drink tonight." He held his thumb and forefinger a fraction of an inch apart before one of his bloodshot eyes, indicating the minuscule amount of liquor he claimed to have drunk tonight.

Penelope cast her eyes quickly about the elegant room. What would happen to this wonderful place when Bradley Fairmount, only son of Lord Bellingsford's late younger brother, succeeded to the title?

"Shall I summon your valet, sir?" she offered.

"Of course not," Bradley declared with drunken bravado. "I shall find my room on my own."

Then he closed his eyes and reeled backward. He caught the back of the chair, desperately clinging to it to retain his uncertain equilibrium.

"I would greatly appreciate your assistance in finding the way to my room," Bradley admitted at last.

Penelope hesitated. Considering how long it had taken her just to find the library, how could she help him find any other room in Bellford Manor?

She studied him as he stood there waiting. If the poor man were so intoxicated that he needed support merely to stand, she reasoned, surely there was no harm merely in helping him to find his own bedchamber, where perhaps he would get the sobering sleep he so desperately needed. Was there?

"Come, sir," she said, offering her hand to him. "Somehow, we shall find your room."

Wrapping his arm about her shoulder, Bradley guided Penelope from the library and out into the corridor. "I believe 'tis in this direction," he said.

Although she gave him what support she could in order for him to remain upright, Penelope felt that she was not helping him, but that Bradley was actually leading her. They mounted a broad flight of stairs and proceeded down another, less well-lit, yet equally elegant, corridor.

"Success at last!" Bradley declared as he drew her to a halt before the door. As he reached for the doorknob, he stumbled forward.

"Steady, sir. Steady," she said, quickly moving in to prevent him from falling over. Suddenly she found herself pinned between Bradley and the door. "Mr. Fairmount, you're very drunk."

She pushed hard against him to free herself. He pressed forward, pinning her hands against his chest. Before she could protest further, he clapped his hand over her mouth. With one deft movement, Bradley opened the door with his free hand. Slowly and relentlessly, he drove her inside. Unable to see where she was going, Penelope stumbled backward into the room. Bradley gave the door a kick. It slammed firmly shut behind him.

"Indeed, I am drunk," he answered her in a voice hoarse with liquor and with lust. He removed his hand from her mouth and seized her in his arms. The reek of alcohol on his breath brought tears to her eyes. "I am drunk with love for you!"

He attempted to lower his face to hers. She turned her head and tried again to push him away.

"Don't be ridiculous, Mr. Fairmount," she scolded with a command she scarcely felt. "You don't even know me."

"Ah, but I do know you, my shy little Penelope," Bradley corrected. "I have seen you serving here before."

The idea of Mr. Fairmount watching her, without her being aware, as she went about her assigned chores at Bellford Manor was decidedly distasteful. Her lip curled with revulsion.

"Each time I saw you, I thought you more lovely than the last," he whispered hoarsely. "I resolved not to rest until I had made you mine."

"Mr. Fairmount, let me go!" she shouted, hoping to draw someone's—anyone's—attention. In this part of the house, she could not hear the music that played loudly in the ballroom. She greatly doubted that anyone there could hear her feeble cries for help. In desperation, she slammed her hands hard against his chest.

He reached up and coiled his fingers tightly about both her hands, trapping them against his chest. His amber eyes studied hers.

'You *must* retain some self-control,' she tried to tell herself. 'You *must* not let him see your fear.'

Nevertheless, she could not prevent herself from shuddering as Bradley raised his other hand to her face. He clumsily slid his hand down her cheek to the small hollow of her throat, then reached behind her neck, pulling out and discarding the pins that held her hair in place. He let the golden strands trickle through his fingers.

Penelope shivered with fear and revulsion.

"How much softer you look with your hair loose," he said. "Much more lovely—more vulnerable."

Despite her continued protests, his hand fumbled over the curve of her shoulder to rest upon her breast. Slowly, he began to lower his face to hers.

She stamped her heavy working shoe forcefully down

upon his elegantly satin-pumped toes. As he reared back, howling in pain, she pushed him away with all her strength.

Falling backward, Bradley grasped at the bodice of her dress. The plain gray wool shredded, revealing her bare, white breasts.

CHAPTER
TWO

THE BOOM OF the door as it slammed against the wall reverberated through the bedchamber.

"Uncle Roger, you old spoilsport!" Bradley complained to the tall, fair-haired gentleman who stood scowling in the doorway. He slapped both fists down upon his knees in frustration.

"Honestly, Bradley. You could at least use your own bedchamber," Lord Bellingsford said scornfully as he strode into the room. His pale green eyes rapidly flickered over Bradley, who was still seated upon the floor. "You look ridiculous. Rise, immediately," his lordship ordered, grimacing with disgust.

Bradley tried to rise, but his legs crumpled beneath him. Only by grasping at the bedcurtains and pulling himself up could he awkwardly manage to stand.

Lord Bellingsford turned to Penelope. Her hands tugged at the shreds of fabric in an effort to keep them together to cover her.

In a gentler voice than the one with which he had addressed Bradley, his lordship asked, "Are you quite all right, girl?"

Befuddled, Penelope merely nodded her response. She shuddered to think what might have happened were it not for Lord Bellingsford's timely intrusion.

"Go to Mrs. Applebottom, the housekeeper," his lordship told her, gesturing toward her rent clothing. "She will help you—"

Lord Bellingsford's hand halted in midair. His fine white eyebrows shot up with surprise. He ran his fingers through his thinning blond hair, which was graying at the temples. Frowning, he peered intently at Penelope.

"B'gads, girl! What have you? Come closer," his lordship said, motioning her toward him. When Penelope hesitated, he insisted, "Come, come. I shan't harm you. I'm not like that one." He jerked his head scornfully in Bradley's direction, then he pointed to Penelope's throat. "But I must see that."

Whatever was his lordship talking about? Slowly, on quaking legs, Penelope approached.

His lordship was staring at the small filigree heart hung from a slender golden chain that Penelope wore about her neck. He raised his eyes to study her face.

Penelope was deeply disconcerted by his lordship's intense scrutiny. She could not quite comprehend the strange expression in his eyes.

His gaze was not coolly disdainful, as was Corbett's. There was certainly none of the lust so apparent in Mr. Fairmount's bold appraisal of her. Penelope was not frightened by Lord Bellingsford's gaze, but his curious expression puzzled her just the same.

"How did you come by this, girl?" he murmured.

Penelope blinked with surprise. No one had ever asked her that question before. Even if they had, she could not have given them an answer. It seemed to her that she had always owned it. She was as puzzled as his lordship as to how the small heart had come into her possession.

'Twas the only piece of jewelry she owned—probably the only jewelry she would ever own. Although she wore it every day, she remembered her mother's warning—*Never let anyone see it, they'd only say you stole it*—so she always kept it tucked beneath her bodice. Only she and her mother knew of its existence.

"I . . . I've always had it, m'lord," Penelope stammered.

Lord Bellingsford shook his head, a look of grim refusal

on his face. "Oh, no. Not this. *This* is a part of the
Bellingsford jewels. I would recognize that piece anywhere." Sternly, he repeated his demand. "How did you
come by it?"

Before Penelope could reply, Bradley declared, "She stole
it!"

"I did not!"

"Then why were you hiding it beneath your clothing?"
Bradley persisted.

"But, Bradley," Lord Bellingsford interrupted, "the girl
does not have the look of your typical thief." His lordship
was still frowning and still boldly inspecting Penelope's
face.

"Aha, Uncle Roger," Bradley declared. "You see how
cleverly these people deceive us!"

"But how do you explain her torn gown, and your own
rather unusual position on the floor when I entered?" Lord
Bellingsford asked, casting Bradley an inquisitive glare.

"That is precisely what the altercation was about."
Bradley staggered to his uncle's side. "I . . . I espied her
skulking about the corridors, prowling into various bedchambers. Suspicious of her behavior, I followed her here,
where I confronted her. When I attempted to apprehend
her—well, you can plainly see with what results," he finished with a disdainful gesture toward the spot on the floor
where he had sat. "The chit knocked me to the floor. Who
knows but she might have killed me with the poker had you
not intervened!"

As Penelope watched Lord Bellingsford's skeptical expression in response to Bradley's preposterous tale, she ex-
perienced a growing feeling of relief. Well, of course, Lord
Bellingsford would believe her. *No one* could believe that
drunken lout Bradley! Penelope felt her first glimmer of
hope since this entire episode began.

Then, in an ominously deep voice, his lordship turned to
her and demanded, "You do know the penalty for thievery,
girl?"

Oh, how *could* his lordship believe Bradley? she silently cried. She had always thought his lordship so kind and fair. How disappointing to discover that Lord Bellingsford would take the part of one of his own against a mere stranger—regardless of right or wrong. She saw her hopes for exoneration quickly disappear.

"Don't you, girl?" his lordship repeated his demand.

Too scared to reply, Penelope nodded silently. Indeed, she did know the penalty for thievery. Who had not seen the corpses swinging from the gallows at the crossroads?

"Shall I see that a footman is sent to summon the constable, Uncle Roger?" Bradley offered, quickly making for the bellpull.

For a man who was so terribly much in love with her only moments ago, Penelope decided, Mr. Fairmount certainly was eager enough now to see her carried off to jail.

Lord Bellingsford pursed his lips and frowned. "I think not," he answered.

Penelope breathed with relief again.

"Surely, Uncle Roger, you do not condone such behavior—especially in the lower classes!"

"I have known this girl and her parents for many years," Lord Bellingsford said. "If she says she did not steal the necklace, I am inclined to believe her. I should like to speak to her parents first, before I consider sending her to prison."

Penelope sat in one of the large, comfortable leather chairs in Lord Bellingsford's spacious study, yet how could she be at ease? She pulled the voluminous shawl that Mrs. Applebottom had loaned her more tightly across her breast. She cradled the knotted ends in her lap and rocked back and forth, as if that would give her some of the comfort she so sorely needed now. The fine leather creaked with each movement she made. She watched the fading firelight flickering across the richly patterned carpet.

'Twas that peculiar time of night when all but the heartiest revellers at Lord Bellingsford's ball had retired to their bedchambers, yet the daytime house servants had not yet risen, once again to be about their daily chores. The house was so quiet that Penelope could hear the chimes of the tall clock in the hallway reverberating all the way down the empty corridor.

Penelope looked across the room to the chair beside the door, where the ample Mrs. Applebottom was ensconced. She estimated that two or three strong men might have difficulty getting past this formidable woman. Did Lord Bellingsford consider Penelope *that* dangerous that he should set her under such a heavy guard?

The creak of the opening door roused Penelope. When she saw her mother follow Lord Bellingsford and Bradley Fairmount into the room, she pulled the shawl high about her neck to conceal her torn clothing. Her mother would be upset enough upon discovering that her daughter was accused of theft. No sense in giving the poor old woman an attack of the apoplexy with the additional worry that her only daughter was running about Bellford Manor half naked.

"Penelope!" Mrs. Graves cried, rushing to her side. Wisps of gray hair fell across her large brown eyes, which were wide with bewilderment. "What happened? What could his lordship want of us at this hour?"

When Penelope opened her mouth to speak, a great lump rose in her throat. All that emerged was a broken gasp. Mrs. Graves wrapped one plump, sagging arm about Penelope's slim shoulders and drew her head comfortingly to her motherly breast.

"Mrs. Graves, I must know." Lord Bellingsford opened his extended hand to reveal the small filigree heart. "Have you ever seen this before?"

Mrs. Graves frowned and examined the delicate ornament. "What is it, m'lord?"

"My necklace, Mama!" Penelope cried.

"Hush, girl. I can see 'tis a necklace." Mrs. Graves turned to Lord Bellingsford and lifted the shiny necklace from his palm. She swung it back and forth so that the delicate gold filigree glittered in the firelight. " 'Tis very pretty. But what has this to do with me and mine, m'lord?"

Lord Bellingsford heaved a great sigh. Gently, he reclaimed the necklace. "Indeed, 'tis pretty. But have you ever seen it before tonight?"

Mrs. Graves was silent for several minutes. She frowned, as if searching for some elusive memory. Penelope could barely breathe, so anxious was she for her mother's crucial reply.

"Think carefully, Mrs. Graves," Lord Bellingsford cautioned her. " 'Tis exceedingly important, for your daughter's sake."

Mrs. Graves shook her head. "No, m'lord," was all she said.

"Mama!"

"Have you *never* seen this in your daughter's possession?" Lord Bellingsford repeated insistently.

Mrs. Graves released a derisive chuckle. "Where would Penelope get such a necklace, m'lord? Unless she stole it."

"Mama!" Penelope exclaimed. Was it the lateness of the hour or the disconcerting circumstances? Why, oh, why did it have to be tonight of all nights that the elderly woman had one of her spells of forgetfulness?

"Where's Papa?" Penelope asked.

Mrs. Graves shrugged her plump shoulders. "Off drinking with his cronies, I suppose," she answered. "Oh, who needs him anyway?"

When Papa went off with his friends, there was no telling when he would return. Penelope sighed. Now she was doomed, for a certainty!

"I shall summon the constable," Bradley quickly volunteered.

"Not yet," his lordship said, raising his hand to stay Bradley's eager rush to the bellpull. "There is one last recourse. I have not yet examined the jewel case."

Lord Bellingsford ordered the square mahogany casket retrieved from its place of security in his bedchamber. Penelope sat, hunched over and silent, in the chair while she waited. Mrs. Applebottom set the case atop the large oak desk in the center of the room. Lord Bellingsford withdrew a small brass key from one of the desk drawers and inserted it in the lock. The tumblers turned with a click.

"It was locked!" Penelope turned to Lord Bellingsford and declared, "M'lord, how could I take the necklace from a locked case?"

Lord Bellingsford frowned and stroked his chin. Penelope began to hope that his lordship might at last see reason. Then he opened the lid to search inside.

"Merciful heavens, just look at it all!" Penelope exclaimed when she saw the marvelous array of precious stones set in gold that sparkled up from the black-velvet depths. "If I were going to steal something from that case, do you think I would settle for a little gold heart?"

Penelope swallowed hard as all eyes turned to stare at her. She had the distinct impression that she should not have said what she said in precisely that fashion.

"There was a set. The one was lost"—his lordship paused to draw in a deep breath, as if continuing was very difficult for him—"many years ago. The other I have kept in here," he explained as, with great care, he moved aside the ropes of lustrous pearls and the brooches encrusted with brilliant stones.

Penelope held her breath and waited.

Lord Bellingsford raised his head to stare at Penelope. "The necklace is gone."

Penelope felt her stomach turn to ice, yet her face and neck grew hot with the realization of the fate that now awaited her.

His lordship once again turned over the jewels. "How curious," he observed. "Nothing else is missing."

"Perhaps that was all she had time to steal," Bradley suggested.

"I did not steal this necklace!"

"Well, now 'tis a matter for the magistrate to decide," Bradley said smugly.

Very slowly, Lord Bellingsford closed the lid of the jewel case and turned to Penelope. Once again he studied her with a frown and that same strange look in his eyes.

"How I wish you could prove . . ." His voice trailed off into a sigh. "What is the world coming to these days when one cannot even trust the vicar's housekeeper?" In a quivering voice, his lordship said, "Under the circumstances, I suppose I have no alternative."

Lord Bellingsford strode to the fireplace and tugged at the tapestried bellpull that hung beside the mantel. The liveried footman appeared almost immediately. Penelope felt her blood congeal in her veins. Even now, she could feel the noose tightening about her neck.

"Summon the constable," his lordship ordered.

Her head spun so badly that she was barely aware of her mother standing beside her, gently patting her shoulder to comfort her. She did not want to be aware of Bradley Fairmount's amber eyes flickering over her from head to toe.

Only vaguely was she aware of Lord Bellingsford handing the jewel case to the housekeeper.

"There is a small tear in the lining," his lordship said. "Please see to its repair, Mrs. Applebottom."

The large woman nodded her compliance.

Penelope paced her small cell at the top story of the old inn—six steps across, six steps back. Even at this distance, she could smell the aroma of frying bacon and freshly baked buns arising from the kitchen far below. She had no taste for food, nevertheless her stomach protested its empty state. 'No use,' she thought. She had no money.

In spite of the large old shawl, Penelope shivered in the breeze that arose with the dawn. She stared at the cold, sooty grate. She had no money for firewood, either. The shawl and the fire were useless anyway, she thought when she realized that her true chill came not from the room nor from the time of day, but from her own inner fears.

She tried to brush her hair back, away from her face. She wished she could have returned it to its customary neat chignon, but Bradley had lost all her pins. The best she supposed she could achieve under the circumstances was a single, neat plait down her back. Even then, with nothing to secure it, every movement caused it to come further undone until, once again, her hair was hanging loose and unkempt.

Penelope had worked hard from sunup yesterday to the very moment she was taken from serving at the ball. She had not been able to sleep a wink last night. She was so tired now that her head drooped. She had to shake her head occasionally to keep her eyelids from closing. Yet one glance at the filthy clump of straw-stuffed mattress ticking lumped in the corner—and the minute creatures crawling through it—made her quickly reconsider ever lying down there to sleep.

She sat upon the small footstool by the window, leaned her elbow upon the sill, and rested her head in the palm of her hand. As the new day dawned, she began to doze.

Her head dropped and slipped out of her hand, bumping against the leaded window mullion. She reached up and gingerly patted the small lump that was already swelling above her right temple.

Penelope stood and began to pace again. How long would she have to remain in jail before she ended her days as just another corpse swinging in the breeze at the crossroads? Or would she be taken to London, to provide the townspeople entertainment dancing the Tyburn jig? Perhaps, considering her otherwise sterling character and the comparatively small value of the necklace, the magistrate might be inclined to leniency and she would only be transported to Botany Bay in far-off Australia where she would never see her mother or father again.

Her poor mother, with her failing memory, had done more

harm than good, Penelope feared. While she knew her father would do all he could to help her, unfortunately not even he was aware that she possessed the necklace. The Reverend Mr. Wroxley might vouch for her character, but oh, how she wished there was some way to completely establish her innocence!

Corbett knew very well he would be suffering this morning from overindulging last night. Even so, seeing Penelope again had prompted his intemperance in the hopes of forgetting her. The throbbing at his temples reminded him that he had not been successful.

The pain was exacerbated by the noisy patter of footsteps down the staircase and across the hall. Even before he saw her, Corbett knew very well which of Lord Bellingsford's guests would make such a noticeable entry.

'Actually, 'tis vastly helpful,' he thought as he heard the footsteps draw nearer. 'One should always be forewarned before encountering the ebullient Miss Margaret Dilley.'

"Good morning, everyone!" Miss Dilley declared cheerfully as she burst into the smaller of the two dining rooms at Bellford Manor.

Mrs. Dilley started, dropping her silver fork noisily upon the delicate china plate. Mr. Dilley choked upon his coffee. Even Lord Ormsley dropped his toast, jellied-side-down, upon the snowy tablecloth.

Corbett was grateful that he had cultivated a stern self-discipline that enabled him to face Miss Dilley's unbridled enthusiasm with a more placid demeanor.

"Now, now, Mama, do not scold," Miss Dilley pleaded, pulling her rosy lips into a pretty little pout. She circled the table, planting a kiss upon both Mr. and Mrs. Dilley's cheeks. "I know I am exceedingly tardy, but 'tis not without good cause. 'Twas such a marvelous ball yesterevening, I fairly danced the night away."

"And fairly wore out a dozen partners, I'll wager," Lord Ormsley added with a chuckle. Then he turned to Corbett, seated two places over, and demanded, "Miss Dilley is quite a lively dancer, ain't she, Corbett?"

"Indeed," Corbett agreed.

'Twas the safest observation he could think to make. 'Twould be exceedingly impolite to call attention to the fact that, on the few occasions he had danced with her—and then only at his father's insistence—Miss Dilley had done severe damage to every toe on *both* of his feet. In fact, after having examined his swollen toes this morning, he considered himself quite fortunate to be able to put his boots on.

Lord Ormsley shook his balding head, turned to Mr. Dilley, and demanded, "What ails this younger generation, Dilley?"

Before that gentleman could respond, Lord Ormsley slammed his fist upon the table, rattling the silverware. "They've no stamina, no bottom!" he declared. "The very things that made, and keep, England great!"

How could anyone contradict him?

Corbett concentrated upon the contents of the plate before him so that no one could see his expression of complete exasperation. Father might accuse him of having no stamina, but at least *he* had a sense of decorum. Decorum was obviously something that Father sorely lacked, as he had been one of the very gentlemen who had continued to dance with Miss Dilley long after the more sensible guests had retired to their bedchambers. Corbett shook his head. Imagine, such behavior in a man Father's age!

"I vow, I am famished!" Miss Dilley declared, making her way directly to the plentiful selection offered on the sideboard.

'How could she be famished?' Corbett wondered. When she had not been dancing last night, Miss Dilley had been visiting the groaning board Lord Bellingsford's talented chef had offered for their delectation in the large dining room.

"Everything looks delicious!" Miss Dilley exclaimed, eagerly surveying the array of dishes set out upon the sideboard this morning.

"Do have a care with your figure, Margaret," Mrs. Dilley warned.

Apparently Mrs. Dilley spoke to no avail, Corbett surmised as he watched the softly proportioned Miss Dilley indicate to the footman her numerous choices from the vast sampling.

Miss Dilley's dark tresses tumbled about her shoulders as she turned quickly toward the dining table. Her bright blue eyes surveyed the assembled company, searching for a vacant place.

"The chair beside my son is not taken, Miss Dilley," Lord Ormsley said, indicating the place between himself and Corbett. "Won't you be seated?"

'Subtlety is not Father's forte, by any means,' Corbett silently observed.

"Yes, *do* have a seat *there*, Margaret," Mrs. Dilley ordered.

Corbett also noted that Mrs. Dilley did not seem to suffer from a surfeit of subtlety either. He did not need to be hit over the head with a brick to realize what his father and the elder Dilleys were about.

Mr. Dilley's fortune was ostensibly derived from shipping during the recent war, although it was rumored that his cargo and its sources would not bear too close a scrutiny by the authorities. Still and all, a fortune as vast as the Dilleys' was one of the primary attributes that Lord Ormsley sought in his future daughter-in-law.

Mr. and Mrs. Dilley did not appear averse to the match, either. When one's only daughter was a viscountess, the origin of one's wealth was a matter easily enough overlooked.

Miss Dilley herself seemed to enjoy Corbett's attentions. On the other hand, Miss Dilley seemed to enjoy the attentions of all the gentleman at this house party.

Apparently the only person with any reservations about the potential union was Corbett himself. The only woman he had ever wanted was back in her parents' humble little cottage this morning, preparing for her day of work at the vicarage.

"I vow, 'twas such a ball!" Miss Dilley continued as she settled her rounded little derriere into the chair between Corbett and Lord Ormsley. The footman placed her full plate before her. "I understand Lady Forbush caught Lord Forbush in the garden, *in flagrante delicto,* with Miss Stamish—"

"Margaret!" Mrs. Dilley exclaimed with horror.

"Scandalous!" Lord Ormsley exclaimed with glee. He leaned closer to her, the better to hear more of the latest on dits. "And him old enough to be her father. Simply scandalous, ain't it?"

"So Lady Forbush sneaked into his lordship's bedchamber and slit all his breeches up the rear," Miss Dilley continued to recount to the avidly attentive Lord Ormsley. "So now he cannot make an appearance until they have been mended. According to my abigail, his valet claims he is no good with a needle, and her ladyship's abigail patently refuses to do it."

"You don't say!" Lord Ormsley lamented with a mischievous laugh. "Serves the old rake quite proper."

"Margaret! Must I scold you again for gossiping with the servants?" Mrs. Dilley demanded.

'Miss Dilley quite rightly deserves to be reprimanded for gossiping with the servants and then continuing to spread the scandalous tales about among the guests,' Corbett silently noted. What a pity he could not control his own father's enormously embarrasing predilection for that same proclivity!

"But if I do not gossip, I shall miss all the exciting news," Miss Dilley pouted as she petulantly stirred about the creamed kidneys on her plate. Then she speared a single kidney and held it up before her. She looked about and grinned knowingly at each one of the guests. "Just as all of you missed the most exciting part of yesterevening."

"What happened, Miss Dilley?" Lord Ormsley eagerly demanded, drawing his chair even closer.

Corbett grimaced at his father's behavior but, again, remained silent. Nothing he could say would do any good, anyway. He returned his attentions to his breakfast.

" 'Twas quite a pity, actually," she began. She popped the kidney into her mouth and chewed thoroughly. All the while, Lord Ormsley waited for her next words. "Late last night," she finally announced, "one of the maids was dragged, kicking and screaming, off to jail!"

"Jail!" Mrs. Dilley exclaimed.

A deep—yet certainly groundless, Corbett reassured himself—foreboding caused his heart to accelerate and leap into his throat. Suddenly, he found himself intensely interested in Miss Dilley's gossip. "Which maid?" he demanded.

"Oh, however can one tell one maid from the next?" Miss Dilley asked.

"Do try to remember," Corbett insisted. "Which maid?"

"Oh, one of the kitchen help, as I recall," Miss Dilley answered with a shrug of her rounded little shoulders. "Hired from the village just for the evening, I understand. Honestly, one would think the housekeeper would check their references better before giving them the position."

"Indeed," Lord Ormsley agreed.

"What did she do to warrant such a fate?" Corbett asked.

"Apparently, she stole some things," Miss Dilley answered. "Money, jewelry, some of the good silver, depending upon whom you ask—"

"Where have they taken her?" Corbett demanded, springing to his feet. He was not ordinarily so rude as to interrupt, but he had no time to waste listening to Miss Dilley's endless, and pointless, chatter.

"To the jail, of course," she answered. Her blue eyes were wide with surprise at Corbett's extraordinary reaction. "Well, where else would they take her?"

"Have my horse brought round," Corbett told the butler.

Slapping the serviette down upon the table, he left the remainder of his breakfast unfinished.

"Honestly, Mr. Remington," Miss Dilley called after him as he strode from the dining room. "One would think she had stolen something of yours, the way you're taking on so. . . ."

CHAPTER
THREE

PENELOPE HEARD THE large iron key grating in the heavy lock. She swallowed hard and turned about, steeling herself for whoever might enter her cell. She just hoped that the executioner had not taken it upon himself to anticipate an unfavorable outcome to her trial and had come to perform his duty in advance.

Slowly, the door swung open.

"Penelope?" Corbett quietly called her name.

She released the breath she was holding.

"Oh, Corbett!" she cried. She was so glad to see a familiar face that she completely forgot all her intentions to remain aloof from him. She sprang from her stool and rushed forward.

Abruptly, she stopped in front of him. What in the world was *he* doing here? Had the high-and-mighty Mr. Remington merely come to gloat over the sorry fate of one of the lower classes?

But the expression on Corbett's face was not one of supercilious self-satisfaction. She was almost tempted to label the look in his eyes as desire, but chased such a ridiculous thought from her head. Had Corbett Remington not made it quite plain that he could not possibly desire her?

Corbett reached out, took both ends of the coarse woolen shawl, and gently drew them together over her breasts. He tied the ends into a little knot, pulled at the fringe to make it neat, then stepped back. He jauntily cocked his head to one side and raised one dark eyebrow, as if to admire his handiwork.

Penelope drew in a deep breath as she realized that, in her flustered state, she had rushed toward Corbett, completely forgetting to cover the damage Bradley had done to the bodice of her dress.

Quickly, she turned her back to him and adjusted the shawl more tightly about her. She could feel the hot color rising to her cheeks. Of course, Corbett had been gentleman enough to cover her quickly, but how much had he seen? she wondered. Just enough, came her own silent answer, to know that she had needed covering.

In another place, at another time, Penelope would have shyly and willingly welcomed Corbett to her bare embrace. But she was a prisoner, an accused felon, and he was a nobleman's son who had merely come to satisfy his morbid curiosity.

"I . . . I am surprised to see you here, sir," she stammered, reluctant to turn to face him again. She raised her hand to wipe away her tears.

"No more surprised than I am to see *you* here," Corbett replied. Then he turned away from her to confront Constable Swift. "Bring Miss Graves a needle and thread," he ordered.

"What do I look like, the village seamstress?" the constable replied in a surly voice.

"Miss Graves' gown needs mending. Surely your wife has thread and a needle," Corbett snapped. He indicated the cold fireplace. "Then see to a fire in here." He kicked at the straw-littered floor with his highly polished boot. "Clear away this filth. And bring Miss Graves some breakfast."

Constable Swift frowned. "See here, Mr. Remington, I'm not one of your father's lackeys to be ordered about. I'm a servant of the Crown, you know."

"Then do your duty by the Crown, man."

"Aye, by the crown, I will," the constable grumbled. He stretched out his grimy hand, palm upward. "All that work'll cost you crowns aplenty."

From his waistcoat pocket, Corbett pulled a handful of coins, jingling them together noisily. Penelope watched Constable Swift's bulging eyes narrow with greed.

Corbett broadcast the coins into the vermin-ridden straw. "You shall have your money—just as soon as you have cleaned this place."

Constable Swift immediately trudged off in search of firewood, food, a broom, and his wife.

Penelope watched in awe as Corbett quite easily commanded the situation, setting things to right. 'And all for me!' she told herself in amazement.

She studied his dark head, his tanned skin, and the fine line of his profile in the dim light of the cell.

Quite suddenly, he turned to her.

She was caught! How could he not know that she had been shamelessly staring at him? She swallowed hard, then managed to regain some semblance of composure.

"How . . . how did you know I was here?" Penelope asked.

"News travels fast," Corbett answered. "Especially bad news."

Penelope nodded. She had heard enough below-stairs gossip not to be surprised that it traveled upstairs with equal rapidity.

"Oh, dear," she lamented. "By this evening, 'twill be all over the village how the sexton's daughter was jailed for theft!" She looked up to him and asked, "That is what they are saying about me, isn't it?"

"I have heard that you stole the Bellingsford jewels, the Bellingsford silver, or the entire Bellingsford fortune," he enumerated her crimes, ticking them off one by one on the upraised fingers of his hand. "It depends upon whom you ask. Quite frankly, the way the tale seems to grow with a life of its own, I marvel that you have not been accused of making off with some of the garden statuary."

"They have exaggerated a bit."

"The tale also goes that you were . . . I believe the exact words were 'dragged away kicking and screaming.' "

Penelope blinked and stared at him with amazement.

Corbett nodded. "I too thought it rather preposterous. You never did impress me as the type of person who, when dragged away to jail, would stoop to kicking and screaming."

In spite of her dire predicament, Penelope grinned.

"Penelope." Corbett stated her name so seriously that she was compelled to lift her gaze to his deep blue eyes. "Why *are* you here?"

She hung her head. "I *am* accused of stealing a piece of the Bellingsford jewelry."

Corbett gave a small chuckle. "Ah, so part of the story *is* accurate."

"But 'tis not *true*!" she protested.

"I have known you for many years. I still believe I know you, Penelope," Corbett said quietly. He shook his head. "You could not possibly steal anything."

"I have been trying to tell them that, but no one will believe me!" she cried with exasperation. So relieved was she that someone was finally taking the time to listen to her explanation that the words came flooding out. "I tried to explain to them I've had it ever since I could remember. Mama is the only other person who knows of its existence, but she did not remember when his lordship asked her. She has become so forgetful of late, I worry sometimes if she will be able to find her way home from the vicarage, even though 'tis only a short way down the road and across a field." Penelope gave a tiny, rueful laugh. "Small wonder that she forgot I had the necklace."

"Necklace?" Corbett repeated. His smooth brow creased into a deep frown. He was silent for what seemed an eternity. "A little gold thing—a small filigree heart, I believe. Is that what you're referring to."

"You know about my necklace?" Penelope exclaimed.

"Of course I do, you silly little goose," Corbett chided her.

" 'Tis the one you always wore, but your mother made you keep it tucked inside your clothing."

"She always said if someone saw a person as poor as I with a necklace that fine, I would be accused of stealing it."

"And indeed, you have been. 'Tis so horrid to realize that Mama is always right, isn't it?" Corbett sympathized.

Penelope cast him a look of chagrin. Then she drew her fine brows together in puzzlement. "But how do you know about—"

"Do you not remember?"

"Of course I do not," she answered just a bit peevishly. "If I had remembered that someone else knew of the necklace, I should not be in this mess now."

"I vow, Penelope, your memory is becoming as erratic as you accuse your mother's of being," he chided her with a slight lift of one fine brow. "Do you truly not remember? You showed it to me years ago, then swore me to secrecy."

"Oh, Corbett, I did!" She reached out to clutch at his sleeve with relief, then clung to him in desperation. "Oh, please! Would you tell Lord Bellingsford that? Please!"

"Of course not," he answered quickly.

Penelope stared at him in shocked disbelief.

"I have sworn an oath of secrecy—"

"Corbett!" she fairly screamed with exasperation. As much as she had once appreciated his lively sense of humor and was glad to see it return, 'twas scarcely the time for it now. She waved her hand through the air in a gesture of dismissal. At a more normal volume, she told him, "I freely release you from your vow."

"Very well," Corbett conceded with a shrug of his broad shoulders. "If you think 'twill serve any useful purpose."

" 'Twill get me out of this horrid jail!" she exclaimed. " 'Tis reason enough."

Was there the barest hint of a smile playing about his lips with his offer to help? Penelope wondered. Perhaps Corbett had not made the complete transformation into a pompous ass after all.

* * *

In spite of the hope of freeing Penelope, Corbett frowned as he left the cell. It had been difficult enough the previous evening to leave her, even when he had believed her safe within the shelter of Bellford Manor. How much more fortitude it took to walk away from her now, knowing that he left her in such cruel circumstances—circumstances that she surely did not deserve!

How frail she looked in the gloom of the dismal little cell. Her pale green eyes held so much fear. Her golden hair, at last released from its severe knot, fanned out about her like a halo, accentuating her fragility and vulnerability.

'How had she got that horrid bump at her temple?' he wanted to know. 'If I ever get my hands on the blackguard who did that to her,' he vowed, 'I shall . . . I shall . . .' He could devise no punishment harsh enough.

Seeing her like that, so desperately in need of protection, Corbett had been sorely tempted to throw to the winds all his resolve to find a wealthy wife. He had wanted to enfold Penelope in his arms and comfort her, then and there!

He had wanted to reach up and caress the wispy tendrils of fair hair that softly framed the oval of her face. He wanted to raise her chin, to gaze into her eyes, and kiss her tender lips.

He wanted to smooth his hand over her cheek, across her throat, and down her shoulder. He had been tempted to cup each softly rounded breast gently in his hands. He certainly had not wanted to pull that shabby shawl together to cover her!

For years he had only been able to imagine what delights lay beneath Penelope's simple clothing. The brief glimpse fate had afforded him had been infinitely more satisfying than anything his poor imagination had ever offered.

Still, he had to cover her. He could never allow himself to take advantage of her in her present troubles. He had to do something to alleviate those troubles, to set things right for her.

How strange—to be accused of stealing a necklace she

had owned all her life. He *knew* she had owned it—and he would tell Lord Bellingsford so just as quickly as possible.

First, he decided, he must take Mrs. Graves back to Bellford Manor with him. Regardless of the woman's fading and often erratic memory, she alone held the answer to Penelope's possession of the necklace. Somehow, he must wrest the complete story from her.

Lord Bellingsford leaned back in his deep leather chair and shook his head. "Corbett, my boy," he began sadly, "I see very little logic in subjecting ourselves once again to this extremely unpleasant ordeal. What reason have you to concern yourself with this matter?"

'What reason, indeed?' Corbett thought. Except that he was in love with the lady accused, and would do everything in his power to free her from that horrid jail. Anything, that is, short of actually lighting a powder keg in the basement—he was no Guy Fawkes. On the other hand, should Mrs. Graves' memory fail once again, he just might resort to such measures. After all, he *was* a man with a mission.

"I only wish to see justice done, my lord," Corbett offered by way of explanation.

"Do you believe I have been unjust?" Lord Bellingsford asked, frowning.

'Oh, you have put your foot in it now, Corbett!' he silently chided himself. 'If you have insulted his lordship, do you think he will ever be willing to listen to you? Think quickly, man!'

Calmly, Corbett replied, "I think there are more possibilities to be explored than have heretofore been considered, my lord."

"I am not a man without the capability of reason, Corbett," Lord Bellingsford continued. He pressed his fingertips together before him, like a little tent. "Yet I hesitate to think. . . ."

"Penelope Graves did *not* steal that necklace, my lord,"

Corbett insisted. "She has had it since we were children. I *know*. I saw her with it."

Lord Bellingsford pursed his lips and frowned with intense concentration. He looked at the bewildered Mrs. Graves, who sat in the chair by the window, staring out at the fluttering leaves.

"We *must* ask her once again, my lord," Corbett said. "Somehow, we must make her remember—for Penelope's sake."

Lord Bellingsford rose and slowly approached the gray-haired woman. "Mrs. Graves," he said, rousing her from her contemplation of the foliage. "Thank you for coming again with Corbett."

"Corbett? Is Corbett Remington here?" Mrs. Graves asked. Her weathered face broke into a broad smile as she looked about, searching every corner for him.

Hoping that this might be the spark which ignited her memory, Corbett declared, "Yes, Mrs. Graves. 'Tis I. Corbett."

Mrs. Graves squinted her brown eyes at him and shook her head.

"You're not Corbett. Corbett is that darling, dark-haired little boy who so loves my gingerbread." She gestured disdainfully up and down Corbett's tall figure. "Not some dark stranger towering over me." She turned to Lord Bellingsford. "May I go home now, m'lord? I really should be making Corbett some more gingerbread."

Corbett shook his head. Mrs. Graves' mind was out wandering again. Heaven only knew if it would return in time to save Penelope.

"Please stay for just a moment longer, Mrs. Graves," Corbett requested. "And do try to remember. How did your daughter come by the necklace?"

"What necklace?"

"B'gads! Why did you even bring her here again, Corbett?" Lord Bellingsford cried at the futility of their situation. "Why did you not bring Mr. Graves?"

"I asked for him, but Mrs. Graves said he was away from home and would not tell me where he had gone," Corbett explained. "She continually insisted that she did not need him—nor want him—to come."

Seeing the once lively Mrs. Graves reduced to this condition caused Corbett's heart to ache. He swallowed hard, knowing that all hopes for Penelope were melting away as rapidly as a light snow in April. However could he exonerate Penelope if her mother was incapable of remembering? Surely, there must be something to be done!

"Perhaps if you showed her the necklace once again, my lord," Corbett suggested.

Lord Bellingsford sighed at Corbett's proposal of repeating the useless gesture. Nevertheless, he withdrew the necklace from the drawer of his large, oak desk. Holding it up by the clasp, the golden filigree heart dangled and swung in the sunlight.

Mrs. Graves shook her head.

Corbett reached out and took the necklace from Lord Bellingsford's hand.

"Please look at this more closely, Mrs. Graves," Corbett said. "And do try to remember."

He crooked his elbow and draped the slender chain over the sleeve of his jacket. The gold heart shone in sharp contrast to the dark green superfine. He approached Mrs. Graves.

Uttering a wistful little cry, Mrs. Graves suddenly reached for the crook of his arm. Taking the necklace, she held it in her arms as if she were cradling a small infant. Gently, she rocked it back and forth.

Mrs. Graves stared into her empty arms and murmured, "Mr. Graves and I were married so long . . . so long without a child."

"Mrs. Graves, whatever are you talking about? If you cannot speak sense, I shan't listen to you," Lord Bellingsford warned.

"Please, my lord," Corbett whispered, fearful that any interruption would shatter the small bit of reality upon which Mrs. Graves still maintained a tenuous hold.

"But she is babbling nonsense," Lord Bellingsford protested.

"At least let her finish, my lord," Corbett pleaded. "For Penelope's sake."

Lord Bellingsford sighed and slapped his hands at his side, but remained to listen to whatever else Mrs. Graves might say.

"Oh, I prayed for a babe for years and years, but none ever came," she continued, oblivious to the interruption. "Then, I was walking home from my work at the vicarage one cold autumn night when I heard a strange cry. Scared me for a bit at first, it did, but then I recognized it for what it was—a babe's cry! I found an overturned carriage. I stopped, of course, thinking I'd try to help any what might have survived. But they were all dead, the coachman, the footman, the nanny, even the pretty lady—all dead but this little babe. She had been protected, when the carriage overturned, by all the soft cushions in her little basket."

Mrs. Graves began sniffing. She dabbed awkwardly at her reddening eyes with the frayed cuff of her brown fustian sleeve.

"Looking back now, I think maybe 'twasn't exactly what the good Lord intended," Mrs. Graves admitted remorsefully. She hung her her gray head low upon her chest. Then she began nodding her head sharply up and down, as if to convince them all of the rightness of her actions. She looked up into Lord Bellingsford's eyes. "But I took it then to be the answer to my prayers. By rights, that babe should have been dead along with the others, but she was saved so I could find her. So I took her, I did, and raised her as my very own."

Corbett suddenly drew in a deep breath. He had been so intent upon listening to Mrs. Graves startling revelation that he had forgotten to breathe. He stared at the elderly woman, astounded by her story. 'Twas more than his poor intellect could take in at one time.

Great Scot! What if Mrs. Graves' strange tale were actually true? What if plain, modest Penelope actually was Lord Bellingsford's long-lost daughter? Corbett had hoped to snatch her from the gallows and return her to the safety of her parents' humble little cottage. How could he have foreseen that his actions would result in moving Penelope from the jail to the manor house!

Corbett felt his heart grow warm and his stomach and shoulder muscles tense at the unexpected, yet certainly very welcome, possibilities that this development opened to him. For the first time in almost four years, he began to feel like smiling again.

Corbett watched Lord Bellingsford to see the likable old gentleman's reaction to this marvelous piece of news. But his lordship was still frowning and shaking his head. Apparently Lord Bellingsford was not as quick to accept this happy event.

In a low whisper Lord Bellingsford asked, "How could you have suddenly appeared with an infant, Mrs. Graves, and no one have thought it odd?"

"You know no one in the village bothers much with Mr. Graves and me, m'lord," she explained with a great shrug of her plump, drooping shoulders. "Why, I could paint my face blue and stick feathers out of my ears and those folks would still pay me no heed."

Lord Bellingsford paced the study floor, raking his fingers through his thinning hair.

"Why did you not come forth with the child at the time?" he demanded.

Mrs. Graves hung her head. " 'Twas selfishness, pure and simple, on my part, m'lord, I'm ashamed to say. I'm a good deal older than your lordship and I thought this babe was my last chance ever to be a mother. But you were a young man then. I thought you'd remarry, have other children—a little boy to carry on the title, instead of just a daughter that wouldn't be much missed. . . ."

"Boy or girl, she was still my child!" Lord Bellingsford shouted, his face livid with rage.

"My lord, do not overset yourself so," Corbett said soothingly. 'Twould be the cruelest trick of fate—not to mention the height of irony—for Lord Bellingsford to drop dead of the apoplexy now, just before he was about to save Penelope.

Mrs. Graves gripped Lord Bellingsford's hand and peered up at him in earnest entreaty. "Please don't be angry with me, m'lord," she begged. "If I hadn't found her when I did, she would have died of the cold or been dragged off by wild dogs and . . . well, I saved her life by taking her. I really did!"

With a visible effort, Lord Bellingsford calmed himself. He swallowed hard and asked, "What of the necklace, Mrs. Graves?"

"God in heaven, Bellingsford!" Corbett exclaimed, unable to contain himself any longer. "What more proof could you want?"

"Don't you see, m'lord?" Mrs. Graves replied. " 'Twas the necklace around the babe's neck."

" 'Tis true, the necklace that my daughter wore disappeared years ago. Anyone might easily have found it lying along the roadside," Lord Bellingsford said. "But I removed the matching necklace from my wife's body and put it away for safekeeping. *That* is the necklace still unaccounted for."

Mrs. Graves looked up at his lordship in surprise. "Why, whatever would Penelope want with *two* necklaces, m'lord?"

Standing close to the door, Corbett could hear the sounds of a great rout. Amidst all the confusion and excitement of these parts twenty-four hours, had the servants all run mad and taken over the premises? Cautiously, Corbett opened the study door.

A startling sight met his eyes. Corbett flung the door open wide.

Bradley and Mrs. Applebottom lay in a tangled heap at the

bottom of the staircase. She was shouting something unintelligible because Bradley's fingers were clamped securely over her mouth. She held a large, dark box under her arm. As the enormous woman attempted to scramble to her feet, Bradley threw his entire body atop her to prevent her from rising.

"B'gads, Bradley!" Lord Bellingsford declared. "Have your perversions degenerated so far as to attack elderly woman—and Mrs. Applebottom, of all people—in broad daylight at the foot of the hall stairs, in plain view of all the other servants? Small wonder 'tis so difficult to keep good help, and the ones that do stay always want higher wages," his lordship muttered. He shook his head in despair. "I am heartily glad the guests are still out in the gardens and cannot bear witness to this scandalous affair! Who knows what increasingly more exciting entertainments they would be demanding afterward?"

With one huge shrug, Mrs. Applebottom shed her unwanted burden, stood, and headed for Lord Bellingsford standing at the study door. Bradley, sprawled upon the floor, crawled after her on his hands and knees, snatching at her skirt and ankles, trying to trip her as he went.

Mrs. Applebottom reached out, grasped Bradley by the collar of his jacket and flung him away from her as easily as she would have discarded an empty bottle. He remained propped against the wall where he had landed, panting for breath.

"You had best hope, Bradley, that they do not hear of your smashing defeat at Gentleman Jack's," Corbett could not resist adding with a hearty chuckle.

Not even out of breath from her exertions, Mrs. Applebottom rushed up to Lord Bellingsford, declaring, "I found it, m'lord! I found it!"

From its place of safety tucked under her arm, Mrs. Applebottom produced the mahogany jewel case.

"I was repairing the tear in the lining, m'lord, like you

told me," she explained. "Look what I found had slipped under the velvet."

She pulled out, by its slender golden chain, a small, intricately designed filigree heart. She offered it to Lord Bellingsford.

His lordship held out his hand to accept the small necklace.

"There *are* two," Mrs. Graves whispered.

"The one I removed from my wife's neck," Lord Bellingsford said, lifting the heart that Mrs. Applebottom had discovered. "And the one from about Penelope's neck." He held its mate up beside it. "Then she *is* my daughter!" he exclaimed.

Bradley's face, recently so red from the exertion of his fisticuffs with Mrs. Applebottom, had drained to an ashen white. Tiny beads of perspiration dotted his hairline and his upper lip. He had managed to stand, but had to lean against the wall for support to remain thus.

"Penelope is your *legitimate*—" Bradley gasped. He had not the breath nor the courage to complete the sentence.

"Have no fear, Bradley," Lord Bellingsford informed him. "Upon my demise, you will still be Lord Bellingsford—more is the pity."

Bradley said nothing. He stumbled away from the wall, shaking his head slowly from side to side. With great difficulty, he mounted the stairs.

"Will you accompany me to retrieve your new-found cousin from the jail?" his lordship asked.

"If you will excuse me, Uncle Roger," he whispered hoarsely, "I do believe I am going to be exceedingly ill today instead."

"I should be pleased if you would allow me to accompany you, my lord," Corbett offered.

Lord Bellingsford smiled broadly at him. "You have done both my daughter and me a great service, Corbett. I should be greatly remiss in my gratitude if I did not grant you this one small request. Come," he invited happily. "And now, if the rest of you will excuse me, I must see my daughter!"

With an exceedingly light step, his lordship strode from the room.

CHAPTER
FOUR

CORBETT WAS GLAD that Bradley Fairmount had not accompanied Mrs. Graves, Lord Bellingsford, and him to see to Penelope's release. He did not care overmuch for the spoiled wastrel's company. He himself would not have missed this ride to free Penelope, not even for the opportunity to wed the greatest heiress in England.

Corbett glanced across to Mrs. Graves. Even in her most fantastic flights of fancy, the sexton's wife probably would never have dreamed that one day she would be riding in his lordship's carriage. Yet here she was, seated beside Lord Bellingsford, rolling into the village in as much fashion as any grand lady. Still and all, he thought with a small chuckle, the woman could not have looked any more uncomfortable had she been traveling on the Mail, outside, naked in a blizzard.

In an effort to console the elderly woman, Corbett leaned forward and said, "Lord Bellingsford will secure Penelope's release, Mrs. Graves. Everything will be all right. You will see."

Mrs. Graves, still staring at her hands in her lap, merely nodded. Given the circumstances, Corbett did not think the woman would have much to say. But he was happier than he had been in a long time. Soon Penelope would be free from her dismal cell and free to begin her new life.

Still, he wondered how they would break the news to Penelope that she was no longer a servant, no longer common, nor even merely gently bred. He wondered how Penelope

44

would react to the fact that she was now an heiress and a genuine lady in her own right?

The carriage traveled far too slowly to suit Corbett. He could not wait to see the expression on Penelope's lovely face when she was told the marvelous news.

More importantly, he could not wait to be alone with her. The barriers that had stood between them were destroyed. Once they were alone, he could at last tell Penelope—and show her—how much she had always meant to him. He could explain to her that his callous behavior had only been meant to lessen her hurt when he was forced to leave her. At last he could please his father by benefiting his family's estates and still have the woman he loved—all quite honorably.

Lord Bellingsford's carriage pulled into the small courtyard of the little country inn. The topmost bedchamber served, infrequently, as the village jail. The few men loitering about all turned with great curiosity as Lord Bellingsford and Corbett descended from the carriage. If Corbett had believed it impossible for anyone there to look more surprised, he was very much mistaken. The men's eyes seemed to fairly pop from their respective heads when Mrs. Graves, dowdy wife of the humble village sexton, also emerged from the elegant carriage.

Constable Swift appeared in the doorway of the inn. He paused long enough to give Corbett a wary glance. In his rush to make himself presentable enough to greet his lordship, the constable had missed a buttonhole. His waistcoat lay crookedly across the front of his broad body as he hurried to Lord Bellingsford's side.

"How can I be of service to your lordship this morning?" he asked Lord Bellingsford as he tugged the edges of his rumpled waistcoat down over his paunch.

"We are here for the release of the prisoner, Miss Penelope Graves," Lord Bellingsford said as he strode toward the inn. He did not bother to pause in the courtyard, but burst boldly into the taproom.

Constable Swift followed closely behind. "M'lord, m'lord," he called breathlessly. "You mean the girl what stole—"

"She stole nothing!" Lord Bellingsford snapped. He did not even bother to turn about to express his displeasure with the constable's false accusations, but continued his march through the smoky little taproom toward the stairs at the side of the large fireplace.

Corbett well remembered the way to Penelope's cell. The horrible image of her fragile beauty, unjustly imprisoned there, would haunt him for the rest of his life. He needed no one to guide him. Nevertheless, Lord Bellingsford was in such a rush that Corbett could only offer Mrs. Graves his arm and follow his lordship's lead.

In a more subdued tone, Lord Bellingsford explained to the constable " 'Twas all a great misunderstanding regarding a small piece of jewelry which Miss Graves has owned her entire life. She did not steal it and must be released immediately."

Constable Swift frowned. "Well, m'lord, I don't know as I can release the chit, even into your custody . . . at least not immediately . . . not without the proper papers. . . ."

"But there are no charges against her, constable," Lord Bellingsford said as he mounted the narrow flight of stairs. "You cannot hold an innocent girl prisoner."

"Well, no, m'lord. I suppose not," the constable reluctantly conceded.

Corbett thought he detected more than a bit of disappointment in the constable's voice—the callous bully!

After a brief pause, the constable swallowed hard and said, "Begging your pardon, my lord, if I might be making so bold as to ask, what made your lordship change your mind about—"

"Well, yes, Swift. You *are* making rather bold with yourself," Lord Bellingsford said. One white brow arched haughtily, but his pale green eyes still twinkled. Without even bothering to acknowledge Constable Swift's abject apologies, his lordship continued, "However, since you so *faithfully* execute your duties year after year—"

"Oh, I do, m'lord! I do!" Swift was quick to proclaim.

"I will tell you," his lordship continued. " 'Tis very simple. Penelope Graves is no thief. She is my daughter."

Swift, his beady brown eyes wide with shock, looked back and forth between Lord Bellingsford and Mrs. Graves. He shook his head and made a sputtering sound of derisive laughter. "Oh, no, m'lord. 'Tain't hardly like you to . . . I mean, you can't mean you and the likes of *her* . . ." He glanced back with intense scorn at the shabby-looking, gray-haired woman at Corbett's side. "Not even twenty years ago . . ."

Corbett caught the constable's shoulder and gripped his sleeve. Drawing closer, he hissed at him under his breath, "Swift, you have a tiny little mind—and what there is of it is filthy beyond redemption!"

"As a matter of fact, Constable Swift," Lord Bellingsford continued with more aplomb than Corbett fancied *he* could have mustered in the face of such boorishness, "your erstwhile prisoner is not Penelope Graves at all. She is Lady Ermentrude Fairmount. As you undoubtedly recall, there was a great deal of confusion regarding the disappearance and presumed death of my infant daughter many years ago. Unbeknownst to us all, Mrs. Graves found the child and saved her life. Unable to determine the infant's origins, she kindly cared for her as her very own daughter all these years, until Penelope Graves' true identity recently came to light."

Corbett released a small sigh of relief. He certainly had to admire Lord Bellingsford's diplomatic talents. Constable Swift and his magpie wife would soon have this tale bruited all about the village. With a few well-chosen words, Lord Bellingsford had managed to allay any suspicions that might have been cast upon Mrs. Graves and avert any scandal that might attach itself to his own family.

At the top of the stairs, Corbett waited impatiently while

Constable Swift clattered through his ring of heavy iron keys to find the one that would unlock Penelope's door and restore to her her freedom.

Penelope sat on the wobbly footstool. The room was some-what cleaner—although she believed that Mrs. Swift's furi-ous sweeping had only scattered the vermin and had not truly exterminated them.

The weak tea, which a slatternly serving maid had brought her shortly after Corbett left, had been bitter, but it was ade-quate for washing down the doughy buns and salty bacon that accompanied it. At least she was no longer hungry.

The fire in the grate was warm enough, she thought, al-though one could scarcely call it cheerful. She debated whether to place another stick upon the dying flames.

No, she decided. If Corbett succeeded in his mission, she would soon be gone from here. No need to waste fuel heat-ing an empty cell. And if Corbett did not succeed? Well, she would have to be frugal with what little she already had. She could not afford to buy more, and she could not continue to accept Corbett's charity—*if* he even continued to offer it.

Thoughts of Corbett Remington caused Penelope to sigh. She rose from her little stool and began to pace the small cell once again.

Corbett had been gone for an interminable amount of time. Had he been able to convince Lord Bellingsford of her innocence? she wondered. If he had, surely they would have come to release her by now. Had Lord Bellingsford been willing to listen once more? Had Corbett even gone to see Lord Bellingsford? Or had he perhaps taken off for London instead—and forgotten all about her once again?

Penelope spun about as the door creaked open.

"Oh, m'lord," she murmured when she saw Lord Bellingsford standing in the doorway. Quickly recovering her senses, she dropped a curtsey.

As she rose, she saw Corbett slowly peek his head into the room. He grinned at her. She drew in a deep breath at the sight of him. She had not forgotten how handsome he was when he smiled. And he had not failed her! She gave him a grateful smile in return. She blushed as she nervously fingered the edges of the hasty stitching she had done to repair her damaged bodice.

From the doorway, Lord Bellingsford spoke to her in a soft, hoarse whisper. "To think that I should be able to hold you at last after all these years!"

Penelope blinked with surprise. Hold her? She had *never* thought Lord Bellingsford a *roué*! She quickly glanced at Corbett. Surely, his lordship would not dare—especially with witnesses!

"My own dear girl," his lordship continued to murmur as he advanced toward her.

Had Lord Bellingsford run mad? she wondered, as feelings of panic grew within her. One occasionally heard tales, although such things were usually well-kept secrets among the upper class. Quite a pity, actually. She had always thought Lord Bellingsford a pleasant, rather sensible old gentleman.

She considered the possibility of fleeing, but the doorway was blocked and, in the tiny cell, there was nowhere else to go. She supposed she could have backed away, but she was afraid to move or even to speak lest the slightest motion set his lordship, in his demented state, off on some lunatic spree. And, as she was two stories up, she had no intention whatsoever of hurtling herself out the window, even to save her honor.

But Lord Bellingsford merely took both of her hands gently in his. Although he held his upper lip rigid, Penelope saw his lower lip begin to quiver ever so slightly and his pale green eyes mist over with tears.

' 'Twould be rather difficult to imprison a person, especially a lord, merely for being eccentric,' Penelope thought. 'If that were the case, half the country could be confined to Bedlam.' She supposed as long as his lordship harmed no one, he might be allowed to roam loose about the village.

With great relief Penelope saw Corbett draw her mother into the now crowded little cell.

"Mama!" Penelope whispered, trying to attract her mother's attention without making any gesture which might upset the delicate balance of his lordship's mind, indeed scarcely moving her lips at all. Her heart ached when she saw the bewildered look on the elderly woman's face and her obvious reluctance to enter the dismal room.

Lord Bellingsford appeared to regain his full self-control. "There had been a grave injustice done you, my dear girl," he explained in his normal voice.

'His dear girl?' Penelope silently echoed. Whyever should he call her that? And "a grave injustice"? Of course she had been unjustly imprisoned, but had he not come to release her? Surely that was sufficient atonement. Why did they not simply open the cell door and let her go? Oh, everything was *so* muddled. She felt as confused as her poor mother seemed to be.

She threw a pleading glance to Corbett. Even though he had not given her any more explanations than anyone else had, somehow his very presence seemed to comfort her. Perhaps, once again, he could help her—this time, to understand what was happening.

But Corbett merely stood in the doorway, grinning. Had he too gone mad? Or was he actually taking some perverse pleasure in watching her puzzlement at the strange scene being played out before her? Either way, Penelope feared she could expect no help from him now either.

"Henceforth, I shall do everything in my power to right that wrong, and to make your life better for you," Lord Bellingsford continued. "And the first thing that I shall do—" His lordship withdrew from his waistcoat pocket the small chain and pendant heart.

"My necklace!" Penelope exclaimed.

"Yes, this truly does belong to you." Lord Bellingsford folded the necklace into Penelope's upturned palm.

"Oh, m'lord, you *do* believe me!" she cried, clutching the necklace to her breast as if she were afraid someone would try to take it away from her again. She turned to Mrs. Graves. "You *did* remember my necklace after all, Mama. You *did* convince them I did not steal it."

Mrs. Graves merely stood there, staring at the filthy little room in complete bewilderment.

"More so than you will ever believe," Corbett answered in her stead.

Penelope regarded him with a puzzled glance. What more could there be to convince them of, other than her innocence?

"You may thank Mr. Remington for jogging poor Mrs. Graves' failing memory," Lord Bellingsford told Penelope.

"Yes, m'lord," she agreed. She realized she would never have had a second chance to prove her innocence were it not for Corbett. She turned to him and murmured, "I owe you a great deal of thanks, Mr. Remington."

Corbett looked intently into her eyes. "If you want me to believe that you are truly grateful," he told her very softly, "you will stop calling me Mr. Remington."

"Mrs. Graves remembered enough to tell us the truth of how you came by the necklace," Lord Bellingsford said.

"The *truth*?" Penelope repeated. The very idea that there was more behind her possession of the necklace than was at first apparent brought chills of apprehension to the back of her neck and down her arms. "What *is* the truth of my necklace?"

"This is not the place to discuss it, my dear," Lord Bellingsford said as he glanced about the dreary cell. He gestured toward the door. "You do not belong here. I shall take you from this miserable place immediately."

"I'm free?" she hardly dared to question Lord Bellingsford lest he prove to be truly mad and suddenly change his mind. Yet as she left the inn, Penelope could finally declare with more certainty, "I *am* free!"

After a sleepless night spent shivering in her cold and lonely cell, Penelope welcomed the morning sunlight that filtered through the orange and gold leaves and warmed her face and body. After her dark, dank confinement, she savored the scent of the last of the summer flowers, the smell of breakfasts cooking over the hearths of the cottages in the village, and even the acrid smell of the horses. Penelope gratefully drew in deep breaths of the sweet fresh air of freedom.

Penelope hesitated before she entered Lord Bellingsford's elegant carriage. Before she sat on the maroon leather seat, she brushed away the remaining bits of dirty straw that still clung to her skirt. The wheels stirred up loose pebbles and puffs of dirt as the carriage rolled away.

"M'lord, I have been patient, but please, now you *must* tell me," Penelope said as she peered at him questioningly. "What is the truth of my necklace?"

Penelope stared in disbelief at the gentleman who sat across from her in the carriage—a nobleman who had just tried to explain to her that *he* was her real father.

She gave her head an emphatic shake. A nervous little giggle escaped her lips. "Oh, no, m'lord, it simply isn't possible. 'Tis some sort of joke you all are playing on me," she insisted, nodding her head as if that would make it so. She looked at Lord Bellingsford from under lowered lids and gave an injured sniff. "Well, I'm very grateful to your lordship for freeing me from that horrid prison, but I never expected that an honorable gentleman such as yourself would stoop to participating in such an awful trick upon a poor innocent girl."

" 'Tis no trick. I am as astounded as you, my dear," Lord Bellingsford assured her. He smiled and patted her hand. "And I am ever so delighted to have found you again!"

Even though Lord Bellingsford's reply had been kind and most sincere, Penelope received no comfort from it. She turned to her mother.

" 'Tis a joke, isn't it, Mama?" Oh, how could she ever become accustomed to the fact that this kindly woman who had cared for her all her life was not truly her mother? She could *never* think of her as anything else.

Mrs. Graves dabbed at her red-rimmed eyes with the sleeve of her brown fustian gown. "We'll miss you, that's certain," she answered with a loud sniff. "But if you were to marry, you'd be leaving us anyway, and at that, only to go to another little cottage just like the one you left. But now you'll be a lady in a grand house and someday you'll marry a lord and have a grand house of your own. 'Tis so much better for you this way, Penelope."

Corbett was still studying her from across the small space between them in the carriage. "If you could but see yourself and Lord Bellingsford as I do," Corbett told her, "you would not doubt for a moment. There is a striking resemblance."

"Your features bear a marked resemblance to my dear departed Natalie, your mother," Lord Bellingsford interjected.

Corbett laughed. "You have not looked in a mirror of late, my lord, not to note that you and Penelope have the same color hair, the same color eyes."

Lord Bellingsford smiled and nodded slowly. He was staring into her face again with the same strange expression he had worn when he had first found Bradley and her in his bedchamber at Bellford Manor. "Seeing you now, I marvel that I never noted the resemblance before, my dear Ermentrude."

"Ermentrude?" Penelope fairly shouted with sheer horror at the very sound. Quickly recovering, she tried to hide her aversion to the awful name—especially since that wretched Corbett had begun to chuckle again.

"*Lady* Ermentrude," Lord Bellingsford corrected.

If the Graves were not truly her parents, Penelope reasoned, she would have supposed that she might have another name, given to her at birth by her real parents. But, oh merciful heavens! The daughters of earls and dukes and such all had names such as Amanda or Melisande or Rowena, did they not? she silently demanded. Why should she alone be cursed with the name of *Ermentrude*?

"*Must* I become Lady . . . Ermentrude?" she asked. She had difficulty even saying the awful name aloud. "I have been Penelope for ever so long—and I am rather accustomed to it. In fact, if you do not mind, I prefer it."

"Ermentrude was my mother's name," Lord Bellingsford said. "Your Grandmother."

"Then I am sorry," Penelope said. Beneath her breath, she muttered, "For her and for me."

"Well, I suppose it would do no harm to call you Penelope from time to time," Lord Bellingsford relented. "But only until you become accustomed to being called Lady Ermentrude. After all, it *is* your proper name."

Penelope reluctantly nodded. Deep inside, she silently vowed, 'No matter how hard I try, I shall never be an Ermentrude.'

" 'Tis the name by which you will be presented at Court," Lord Bellingsford told her.

"Presented at Court?" Penelope echoed. "Am I not a bit old for that sort of—"

Lord Bellingsford pressed his lips together and frowned. "Well, perhaps, I had not considered . . ."

"Your age does not signify," Corbett told her. From across the shadowy interior of the carriage, his eyes met hers and held her gaze. " 'Tis your position as his lordship's daughter that must be acknowledged. And, even if you are *dreadfully* old," he added with a grin, "in a gown of white, I think you will look a veritable angel—far superior to any other lady there, regardless of her age."

"Corbett is correct," his lordship declared boldly.

"Ermentrude, you have been deprived of so much in your life."

"I have never felt . . . deprived," she said. 'Except perhaps,' she silently, and sadly, amended, 'where Corbett Remington was concerned.'

"I intend to see that you begin to receive immediately all the things you have been missing," his lordship continued, so busy with his plans that he was oblivious to any protest that Penelope had made. "You will live with me now at Bellford Manor, which is your rightful place as my daughter. For the Season in London, we shall remove to Bell House in St. James. I shall obtain for you a voucher to Almack's. As my daughter, those old dragons are certain to accept you—although I daresay you might find the place dreadfully dull. And be certain to eat *before* you go there," he suggested in a conspiratorial whisper. In a normal tone of voice, he assured her, "I am confident, however, that you will find shopping in Bond Street much more to your liking."

Listening to his lordship rattle on in unbridled enthusiasm, Penelope began to think that perhaps what had happened to her was not so horrible after all.

'Twas one thing to be told the truth of one's parentage. Penelope was not so naive that she did not realize that there were probably more people than one would suppose who were actually the offspring of Lord Somebody-or-Other. But 'twas another, entirely different matter to have an earl come to your prison cell, declare you his *legitimate* daughter and heiress, and whisk you off to live a life of luxury and privilege in his magnificent mansion. 'Twas almost as if, suddenly, all her wildest, most fantastic, most frivolous dreams were at last coming true.

"You will be happy, Penelope," Corbett told her. He reached across and gently touched her hand. " 'Twill be so much better for you this way. Trust me."

Penelope considered Corbett's words. If anyone in this

carriage should know what it was like to rise from poverty to
the peerage, 'twas he. Perhaps he *was* correct. She just
hoped that, unlike Corbett Remington, this sudden elevation
of her station in life did not put her in danger of becoming a
pompous ass.

CHAPTER
FIVE

BRADLEY, A HALF-FULL snifter in one hand, paced his bed-chamber. As he seriously doubted that one drink would be enough to offer him the sort of comfort he needed in these trying circumstances, he carried the full crystal decanter in the other hand. He examined the contents of the rather inadequate-looking container and wished he were strong enough to carry the entire cask up from his uncle's cellars.

His head pounded and his stomach churned. He could not decide whether to spend the day drinking his troubles into oblivion or retching into the chamber pot. Considering the way he felt, he would probably be doing a great deal of both.

"You look like hell, sir," his valet observed.

"You need not be so crude, Jakes," Bradley said. "Nor so accurate. My bedchamber is equipped with a mirror." He shot back the contents of the glass, then just as quickly re-filled it.

"Can't be due to the quality of the brandy," Jakes contin-ued, cautiously regarding Bradley from out of the corner of his eye.

"My uncle stocks only the very best," Bradley responded, "regardless of the cost."

" 'Tain't the quantity, neither," Jakes said. "I've seen you down far more than this of an evening."

"And I've suffered no ill effects, either," Bradley stated proudly. "At least none that I was able to discern."

"Could it be—just perhaps, sir—that the rumors I've

57

heard regarding one Penelope Graves, what works as kitchen help from time to time—"

"How *dare* she turn out to be my long-lost cousin!" Bradley demanded angrily. The blue veins at his temples bulged with each syllable he shouted.

He made to take another swallow of the strong brandy, but in his agitated state, he stopped, lowered the snifter, and just stared into the pier glass.

"What am I to do, Jakes?" he cried. "I was but a child when Aunt Natalie died, and that mewling little brat with her—or so everyone thought. Even then, I hoped Uncle Roger would never remarry. When he did not, I thoroughly enjoyed the prospect of one day succeeding to the earldom. I was especially counting upon my inheriting the sizable Bellingsford fortune."

"As are your many creditors, sir," Jakes observed with a wry twist of his lips.

"Unfortunately, the Bellingsford fortune is derived not from the land itself, but from the personal fortunes of the ladies that the previous earls had the great wisdom to marry," Bradley explained. " 'Tis not entailed with the rest of the estate, but bequeathed to the direct descendant. While I shall inherit the title, Penelope will now inherit the income." Bradley whirled about and smashed the empty snifter into the fireplace. "Jakes, I am ruined!"

"In that case, sir, shouldn't you be taking better care of your possessions?"

Bradley scowled at his valet. The man was insolent, no doubt. But the feisty little fellow *was* just the type of protection Bradley could depend upon in some of the gaming hells he frequented. He supposed he could tolerate the man's impertinence a bit longer.

Bradley tipped back the decanter and drank.

Jakes frowned and pursed his thin lips. "Let's hope your creditors don't discover this unpleasant fact too soon, sir."

"Oh, I harbor no such delusions, Jakes," Bradley said, dropping wearily into a nearby chair. He shook his head.

"Knowing how news circulates, they *will* find out soon, far too soon for my comfort."

"Or, just possibly, for your health," Jakes muttered. More loudly, he inquired, "Will you be fleeing the country, sir? Shall I pack?"

Bradley shook his head, not because he was refusing to flee, but rather because he had no idea at the moment of what he *did* intend to do. " 'Tis difficult enough to get by without funds in England. How much more difficult will it be in some wretched foreign place? No, that is not the answer."

As Bradley contemplated his alternatives, and the new-found cousin who made his choice of one of these alternatives an imperative, he slowly began to smile.

She was a comely enough little wench, with her pale green eyes and soft blond hair. Her slender, softly curving body promised great delights for the lucky man to whom she would offer it—or to the man bold enough to take it.

He pulled himself up sharply. He had enough trouble already, without the additional problems that line of thinking would bring him. But these wild thoughts did lead him to a far more subtle solution to his predicament.

"Jakes, I believe I have struck upon the perfect solution." He held his snifter aloft, as if toasting his own brilliance. "I know how to have the title, the fortune, *and* my delectable little cousin, all at the same time."

His valet regarded him skeptically. "And what might that be, sir?"

"I shall simply have to convince her to marry me."

Jakes regarded his master's rumpled hair, bloodshot eyes, and soiled cravat. "Oh, how could she refuse you, sir!"

Lord Bellingsford's carriage stopped to deliver Mrs. Graves to the sexton's modest cottage. Penelope wrapped a few things into a large woolen shawl, and after a tearful leave-taking, reluctantly continued on to Bellford Manor. Corbett and his lordship's reassurances had made her begin to feel increasingly excited at the prospect of her new life as Lady

Ermentrude. But as each turn of the wheels drew her nearer to Bellford Manor, Penelope believed that the butterflies, which had been excitedly beating in her breast, had descended to her stomach and had transformed into fire-breathing dragons, each on a furious rampage.

The fact that she looked a wretched mess did not help matters either. Oh, Corbett had seen her looking worse. As children, they had romped together through a goodly number of haymows, as well as their fair share of mud puddles after a storm. Still, she wished he could see her looking much better than she did now. She especially hated to think of arriving at Bellford Manor in this state! Perhaps Lord Bellingsford would allow her to enter unnoticed and retire to a small bedchamber to tidy up. The carriage entered the gate and rolled along the smooth, tree-lined drive of Bellford Manor.

However would she find her way about this place? she began to worry. She was quite certain she would still succeed in losing herself again in the vast labyrinthine corridors. Unless, of course, by becoming Lady Ermentrude, she suddenly, miraculously, would have imparted to her some arcane knowledge of how to navigate those puzzling corridors. Perhaps that was how the rest of the lords and ladies did it, she speculated.

She swallowed nervously. 'Twas one thing to serve at Bellford Manor. 'Twas a completely different matter to be acting there as her father's hostess.

With increasing apprehension, Penelope watched the massive structure rise above her. She had never before approached Bellford Manor from the front entrance. She had never drawn near it in an elegant carriage either. She briefly considered leaping from the carriage and, if she had not broken any bones, running all the way back home and trying to forget any of this had ever happened.

But when she saw the tall windows gleaming from the rosy brick facade in the bright morning light, Penelope began to feel all her fears slipping away. 'Twas a beautiful building, inside and out, and, at the moment, Bellford Manor *did* look rather warm and inviting. It might be pleasant to live here after all, she decided.

Surely, 'twould be very pleasant to remove the filthy, ragged dress that she had worn for two days now, and bathe away the grime and stench of that horrid jail, and change into the clean blue fustian gown she had brought with her from the cottage.

But her hopes for an unobtrusive entrance quickly evaporated when she saw the entire staff of Bellford Manor—from Mr. Solloway, the haughty butler, all the way down to Pansy, the youngest and extremely shatter-brained scullery maid—lined up before the entrance, eagerly awaiting presentation to the new Lady Ermentrude.

Seeing them, Penelope began to brush at her skirt and pat at her hair yet again, although she knew it did no good at all. Her hand rose to her mended bodice. Her fingers traced the stitches she had made, ascertaining that none had come undone.

Corbett reached out and took her hand. She drew in a deep breath as he touched not only her fingers, but also brushed against her breast. He slowly lowered her hand to her lap.

"Everyone knows you have been through quite an ordeal, Penelope. No one expects you to look as if you just left the modiste's," he reassured her quietly. Then, more sternly, he scolded, "At any rate, Ermentrude, a *lady* never fidgets."

Penelope grimaced at Corbett's use of her new name. Why was he deliberately calling her that when he must know how she detested it? He must also know perfectly well that she had no idea whatsoever what a lady did—or never did. When she turned to him and saw the mischievous twinkle in his deep blue eyes, she could not help but return his smile. He had intended no harm with his advice. Having helped her escape from prison into a new life, he was now preparing her to enter that life.

With the footman's assistance, Lord Bellingsford alighted

from the carriage. Much to her consternation, he stood in front of the long line of servants, waiting for her to alight.

Penelope remained in the carriage.

"You may come out now, Ermentrude," Lord Bellingsford said.

Penelope began twisting her hands in her lap.

"I must present the servants to you," Lord Bellingsford insisted, raising his voice ever so slightly for it to carry into the recesses of the vehicle where Penelope hid.

" 'Tis customary," Corbett whispered in her ear. "I shall stay with you—if you want me."

Of course she wanted him to stay with her—and not just for this brief entrance into Bellford Manor! She had always wanted him to stay with her. Yet, even with Corbett's reassuring presence, Penelope could not bring herself to make that first bold step out of the dark shelter of the carriage into the sunlight and her brand new life.

"You must go, Penelope," Corbett said, motioning for her to leave.

She began to rise, then quickly sat down again and huddled in the corner. She cast him a pleading glance. "Oh, Corbett, I simply cannot!"

"You can and you will. You *must*," he told her firmly. " 'Tis your duty."

"Duty," she repeated. "Oh, what do *you* know of duty?"

Corbett regarded her silently in the darkness of the interior. "Someday, Penelope, I shall tell you," he answered. "Someday soon."

Penelope turned from him to watch the line of people waiting for her. She was not particularly interested in them—she had seen them enough times before—but she would do anything to break the strange gaze with which Corbett held her.

"But I feel so foolish!" Penelope protested. "I already know them, and they all know me."

"They know you as a fellow servant," Corbett corrected her with a little grin. "Someone with whom they have worked, even as someone whom, from time to time, they have ordered about. Now they must begin to think of you as the person you truly are—Lady Ermentrude Fairmount, someone whom they are to serve and to obey."

"Obey?" she asked incredulously. "I have never even had a dog to command, much less servants to order about." She gave an embarrassed little giggle.

Corbett chuckled too. Then he abruptly rose from his seat and left the carriage. At the foot of the folding steps, he turned back to her. In the sunlight, his eyes appeared even more blue as he watched her, and waited. "Come, Penelope," he said as he extended his hand to her.

When he looked at her that way, Penelope could completely forget that he had ever hurt her. She would go with him into Bellford Manor. Indeed, casting all cares and duties aside, she would willingly go with him anywhere he wished. She took his hand and stepped down.

Corbett handed her into Lord Bellingsford's care. His lordship conducted Penelope down the long line of house servants, presenting each one to her. She was quite unprepared to be greeted with a respectful "m'lady." However, passing the long row of maids, she could not help but notice the sidelong glances and one or two quiet snickers behind her back after she had gone on to the next person in line. Even if she did not think of them precisely as friends, at least she had thought of the people with whom she worked as civil. Even if they thought her ridiculous for taking on grand airs, could they not at least pretend to wish her well? How could they be so cruel as to ridicule her openly now?

'Still, I can hardly blame them,' she thought. 'At the moment, I most certainly do not look like a lady.' She lifted her hand to her hastily mended bodice. Then, remembering Corbett's admonishment, she restrained her impulse and quickly dropped her hand to her side and continued to nod politely.

For years, her family had been the brunt of many a schoolboy's prank, but she had learned to hide her anger. Having

been disappointed in love, she had learned to hide all other
emotions as well. She now exerted all the self-control she
had learned over the years. She would never allow these
people to see how their mockery hurt her now.

At last, the ordeal was finished. Penelope pursed her lips
and frowned as she watched several of the scullery maids
clamp their hands over their mouths and scatter, giggling. As
Lord Bellingsford led her into the house, Penelope allowed
herself to sigh with relief.

"Come with me, if you please, m'lady," Mrs.
Applebottom said. She took Penelope's burden, then led her
across the large marble hall, up a wide flight of stairs, and
down a lengthy corridor.

'Oh bother!' Penelope thought with annoyance as she
watched Mrs. Applebottom's competence in navigating the
corridors. 'It has nothing to do with having a title. Now I
shall be truly lost in this house!'

Mrs. Applebottom stopped before one of the innumerable
doors and pushed it open. Penelope tentatively stepped inside.

"Your suite, m'lady," Mrs. Applebottom explained.

" 'Tis lovely," Penelope said, admiring the gold and white
appointments of the large, elegant bedchamber.

"I'll have your bath prepared, m'lady," Mrs. Applebottom
said. She emptied Penelope's bundle onto the bed. Disdainfully, she picked through the clothing. "One of the chambermaids will assist you until a proper abigail from London can
be engaged."

A chambermaid brought in a large bath mat and placed it
on the floor near the fire, then arranged a large, ornate Chinese silk screen around the mat. Another chambermaid laid
out small, scented soaps and several large, fluffy white towels. Two footmen hauled a large circular tin tub into the
room and placed it upon the mat. A parade of chambermaids
emptied bucketfuls of steaming water into it until the tub
was full.

After they had all left, Penelope wasted no time in strip-

ping off her grimy gown and old cotton chemise and im-
mersing herself in the warm water. Quickly, she washed
away the dirt and stench of the jail with the small, jasmine-
scented soap. After she had rinsed, she enveloped herself in
one of the large towels.

"What shall I do with your clothing?" Mrs. Applebottom
lamented.

She was not asking Penelope. Penelope had the distinct
impression the housekeeper already knew what she intended
to do with the ragged gowns. She was merely talking to herself.

Mrs. Applebottom shook her graying head with dismay as
she held up, by the corner of the collar, the filthy gown that
Penelope had shed. Then the housekeeper tossed it disdainfully onto the floor.

"I brought another," Penelope suggested, gesturing to the
very similar blue fustian gown she had placed on the bench
at the foot of her bed.

Mrs. Applebottom picked it up. She closely scrutinized it,
and obviously found it greatly wanting. "His lordship would
have an attack of the apoplexy—not to mention having *my*
head on a platter—if I allowed you to be seen in this horrid
thing! Especially tonight!"

She turned to Penelope, frowning as she assessed her figure. "We might find one of the chambermaids your size, but
they surely have nothing suitable for a lady to wear either."
She shook her head. "Somewhere, in this large household,
there must be something appropriate for you."

Unable to offer any possibilities, Penelope merely
shrugged.

After a pause, Mrs. Applebottom's face brightened with
sudden inspiration. "Perhaps some of Lady Bellingsford's
old gowns were stored in the attics!"

Penelope wanted to protest. How could she wear a gown
of her dead mother—the mother she had never known?

"They would be dreadfully out of fashion, but perhaps
one could be quickly redone for tonight, and the rest later,"

Mrs. Applebottom speculated. She nodded toward the small clothes that Penelope had also brought with her. "I don't see how you can help but wear these, for the time being. Why don't you put them on while I see to . . . oh, there must be some sort of gown suitable for you!" the rotund housekeeper cried in despair. She hurriedly bustled from the bedchamber.

Alone for the first time since receiving her startling news, Penelope collapsed into a nearby chair. She closed her eyes and drew in several long, slow, deep breaths. She was afraid now to open her eyes, afraid that when she did she would still be in her wretched prison cell, and that all this had been merely a fantastic dream.

Penelope smiled when she opened her eyes and found she was still a very definite part of this elegant new world. She snuggled down deeper into the plush cotton velour upholstery of the chair and pulled the thick, lavender-scented Turkish towel closer about her. Everything here was soft and sweet. Perhaps her life at Bellford Manor would be good after all.

"Quickly! I haven't much time!" the unknown young lady exclaimed as she burst into Penelope's bedchamber.

Penelope started and pulled the towel closer about her.

"Oh, I am so sorry if I startled you," the dark-haired young lady apologized with a loud laugh. She closed the door tightly behind her and leaned against it, as if trying to keep out whoever might be trying to get in. "I realize I should have knocked. 'Twas ever so rude of me. But if I had knocked, 'twould have made a noise."

Penelope thought that no noise short of the crack of doom could be louder than this unknown young lady.

"Then Mama would have found me!" The young lady's blue eyes were so wide with feigned horror that Penelope could not help but laugh. "Mama said I must not be over-curious, but must stay in the drawing room, playing cards with the rest of the guests. Do you know how to play cards?"

Penelope shook her head. Card games—indeed, all games of chance—had never been allowed in the vicarage.

Before Penelope could respond, the young lady continued to rattle on. "I adore playing cards—especially when I am winning. Still, I passed it all by, just to come here to see *you*."

Penelope felt as if she could have passed up this rather dubious honor from this garrulous stranger.

"Mama said 'twould be unseemly for me to come here," the young lady told her. "Still, I just had to come see the scullery maid who turned out to be Lord Bellingsford's long-lost daughter. Oh, I vow, 'tis even more exciting than a romance novel!"

"Well, now you see me," Penelope said. "Are you disappointed that I do not have two heads or three eyes?"

"Oh, I never thought you did," the young lady answered, waving her hand as if to dismiss the very ridiculousness of Penelope's suggestion. She began to circle Penelope, boldly assessing her. "Actually, you are a rather pretty little thing at that." Then she walked to the gown which lay discarded upon the floor. "Whatever in the world is *this*?" she demanded.

"My gown," Penelope answered.

The young lady gave it an exploratory nudge with the toe of her elegantly slippered foot. "Why, fancy that! So 'tis. Well, indeed, all things considered, right now, I think that you present far more of a challenge to me than any mere card game."

Penelope fought down the urge to do bodily harm to the overly frank young lady.

"Well, it does not signify after all," the young lady continued to rattle on, obviously unaware of Penelope's plans for her ultimate demise. "Wait right here."

Penelope glanced down at her own figure enveloped only in the large Turkish towel. "I do not think I will be going anywhere," she assured her.

"Good. I have just the thing for you," she threatened as she opened the bedchamber door and peeked out into the corridor.

She glanced left, then right—most probably, Penelope thought, making certain that 'Mama' was not searching for her. Then the young lady slipped out the door, slamming it shut behind her. If this girl were ever called upon to act the spy for England, Penelope decided, Bonaparte would surely win this war.

The room was extraordinarily quiet after the young lady left. Penelope still had no idea who she was, but she was almost sorry to see the lively creature leave. And the peculiar young lady had said she was returning!

If she was, Penelope had to make certain that she was decently attired this time. She took a deep breath and sprang from the chair. She barely had time to don her clean cotton shift before the young lady burst in again. This time she was followed by her mousy-looking abigail, who was burdened under three gowns. The abigail placed the gowns on Penelope's bed.

The young lady indicated the discarded gown to her abigail. "Take this thing and burn it," she ordered.

"Oh, no, not my gown—" Penelope began to protest.

"Oh, hush," she said. " 'Tis not as if you will ever actually be wearing that thing again. 'Tisn't even fit to pass on to the servants. Anyway, I am sure your father will be buying you all sorts of new things. But," she said, turning to the gowns on the bed, "right now, you are in dire need of *my* services."

"But who *are* you?" Penelope finally found the opportunity to ask this forceful young lady.

"Oh, how silly of me not to tell you! My name is Margaret Dilley. My parents and I are Lord Bellingsford's house guests, so I suppose we shall be seeing quite a bit of each other for the next fortnight. Won't that be grand?"

Unable to make any reply that would be considered polite, Penelope merely nodded.

"Now, come see what I have for you," she invited.

Rising from her chair, Penelope cautiously approached the bed. She lifted the hem of the gown closest to her—pale blue, like the sky on a spring morning. It felt as light and as soft to her touch as any cloud could ever be.

"Silk," Margaret said. "Lovely, isn't it? Just the thing to wear for dinner this evening."

" 'Twould be just the thing to wear to Heaven," Penelope heartily agreed.

"The only trouble is, already 'tis just a bit too snug for me across the bodice," Margaret complained. " 'Tis all Lord Bellingsford's cook's fault, you know."

Surreptitiously examining Miss Dilley's voluptuous figure, Penelope was not so certain the cook should shoulder all the blame, but she nodded her tacit agreement anyway.

"At any rate, I am lending these to you until you can have some new gowns made in London."

Stunned by the complete stranger's kindness, Penelope could only murmur, "Oh, how can I ever thank you?"

Margaret laughed and waved her hand through the air. "Oh, they did not fit me, and I am only lending them to you anyway, so you needn't take on so."

Seeking refuge behind the large Chinese screen, Penelope slipped the blue silk gown over her head. Margaret began to do up the numerous small pearl buttons at the back.

"Well, you are a bit taller," Margaret said, stooping to examine the hem. She tugged at the excess fabric at Penelope's sides. "A bit thinner, too. Still, 'tis nothing that a competent seamstress cannot easily remedy."

Margaret's abigail was immediately pressed into service.

"Oh, I wish I could stay to watch the transformation," Margaret lamented. "But Mama will never believe I needed to be in the necessary this long—and if I tell her the truth, there will be no end to her scolding."

"But, your mother *will* know," Penelope protested. "Will she not recognize your gown?"

After only a moment's pause, Miss Dilley answered, "No," most emphatically. "I have so many things, 'tis difficult to keep account of them all. And at any rate, Mama only keeps her eagle's eye on *me* and what *I* am up to, not my clothing."

Penelope released just a small giggle.

Somehow, she did not believe Mrs. Dilley's scolding would have any effect whatsoever on Margaret.

At Miss Dilley's second departure, the room was once again plunged into silence, except for the quiet stitching of the mousy little abigail. Penelope fancied Miss Dilley consistently entered and exited with much the same abruptness.

While Penelope waited, the abigail quickly stitched a seam up the loose fabric under Penelope's arms.

" 'Tis finished, m'lady," the abigail said. Then she, too, left Penelope alone in the large and now rather lonely bedchamber.

CHAPTER
SIX

AFTER SHE HAD brushed the straw and tangles from her hair, Penelope waited for a bit, uncertain what to do next. Her stomach had begun to protest hours ago. She realized she had not eaten since early that morning, and then only sparingly due to the abysmal quality of the food at the inn and her own nervousness. She *must* go downstairs, not only for the sake of her poor, desperate stomach, but for the sake of Lord Bellingsford as well. She was his daughter, and prepared or not, she must prove herself equal to the task.

She opened her bedchamber door and peeked out. On either side, the corridor extended in vast, unmarked stretches. Penelope felt as desolate as if she had been abandoned upon the frozen Russian steppes.

'Oh, I cannot do this!' she silently wailed as she again envisioned descending to the drawing room and meeting all those strange people, dining with them, actually conversing with them. Then she recalled Corbett's heartening words. 'You can. You must,' she repeated to herself. ''Tis your duty.' She might not know anything about being the daughter of an earl, but the necessity of performing one's duty was something that Penelope did understand.

She ventured out into the hall. She debated whether or not to close her bedchamber door behind her. Once closed, if she lost her courage and decided to return to the haven of her bedchamber, she might never find it again amongst all the other identical doors.

71

'No,' she decided. 'There must be no turning back.'

With a decisive click, she closed the door and proceeded down the corridor. She found a staircase of several flights that wound about a single tall newel post. Well, 'twas easy enough to decide which way to go to reach the ground floor. But the twists and turns of the numerous corridors still confused her. She passed through rooms of furniture, paintings, and statues that looked vaguely familiar. She assumed they were the rooms she had passed through while searching for the library yesterevening—or while trying to assist Bradley Fairmount in their ill-fated search for his bedchamber.

'Twas as if the very thought of Bradley had conjured him up, like some evil jinn. He stood blocking her way down the long, mirrored gallery.

"Are you lost, little cousin?" he asked, smiling.

Penelope's heart jumped from her breast to flutter in her throat. Heaven help her! In her excitement at being brought to live at Bellford Manor, she had completely forgotten that she would now be living under the very same roof as this odious man! Now there truly would be no escaping him. Penelope could only fervently hope that he would soon tire of life in the country and return to his gambling in London.

"No, I am not lost," she managed to answer him calmly. She abruptly turned her back on him and walked quickly down the candlelit corridor, hoping to reach the safety of the crowded drawing room before he caught her.

"Penelope, wait!" he cried.

She could hear his boots clicking along the floor as he pursued her. The skin on the back of her neck prickled as she felt him drawing ever closer.

Increasing her pace, she called back over her shoulder to him, "I have nothing to say to you, Bradley Fairmount."

"I am not asking you to say anything, but surely you can at least listen to my apology," he pleaded.

Penelope could tell by the sound of his footsteps that

Bradley had stopped his pursuit. She took refuge behind a gold damask-covered sofa and turned to face him. Her hands gripped the back of the sofa until her knuckles were quite white. She raised her chin and squared her shoulders. "An apology?" she demanded.

"Allow me to explain." Bradley began to move toward her.

"Do not come one step closer!" she warned, holding him off with a single index finger, pointed directly at his heart as if it were a sword. "If I only need listen to you, then I can hear you very well from where you are." She tried to sound brave, but she knew her voice was quivering as she continued, "And I am warning you, if you attempt to bother me again, this time I shall tell my father. I am not afraid of you any more, Bradley."

He remained where he stood, his fair head hung down upon his chest, his amber eyes lowered in abject penitence. "I assure you, Penelope, you never had any reason to fear me, nor do you now."

She merely frowned at him skeptically.

"Oh, I do not blame you if you do not trust me," he conceded. "'Tis well known that I travel in rather disreputable circles. Sometimes I drink too much and am not in full control of my actions."

"I do not believe that for one moment, Bradley," she said. "I think you knew perfectly well what you were doing."

Bradley stared at the floor. "I am dreadfully ashamed of my despicable behavior toward you, little cousin," he said. "The only excuse I can offer is that, from the first moment I saw you, I was so totally overwhelmed by your loveliness that I could only pursue you."

"You tormented me the way you did because you say you *love* me?" she demanded incredulously. "Do you honestly expect me to believe that, too?"

"I should have known that a young lady of your delicate sensibilities would be offended by such brazenness," Bradley replied. He held his arms outstretched to her.

"Sweet Penelope, can you forgive me? Can you ever think well enough of me to allow some hope to remain in my heart that one day you might return the deep affection I feel for you?"

"But *you* were the one who wanted to summon the constable!" she protested. "You tried to have me sent to jail. You succeeded!"

"It may have seemed that way to you, but I only wished to have the constable investigate the matter more fully," Bradley calmly explained. "It all went so wrong."

Could she trust him after the torment he had put her through? After all, his excuses seemed somewhat plausible. He was behaving himself now. She could not recall any gossip about Bradley that was truly horrid. And he *had* been awfully drunk last night.

After a moment's consideration, she replied, "I . . . I shall have to think about this, Bradley."

"I understand your reluctance, Penelope," he conceded. He offered her his elbow. "Will you at least trust me enough to allow me to conduct you to the drawing room?"

Penelope shook her head. "No. Thank you anyway. If I am to find my way about this place, I must learn to do it on my own."

"Then may I accompany you while you explore?" Grinning sheepishly at her, he raised his hand as if taking an oath. "I promise not to utter a single word that might give away the proper directions."

Penelope eyed him cautiously. 'Twas true, he no longer reeked of alcohol, although she supposed that the scent of Eau de Cologne that furiously assailed her nostrils was doing a great deal to disguise his recent encounter with a more potent liquid. Still, Bradley was able to stand upright on his own, she observed. And, she supposed, no matter when he stopped drinking, 'twould probably take a good bit of time before his bloodshot eyes returned to their normal color.

"Well, if you wish to, I truly do not see how I could stop you," she said as she began walking down the corridor.

Much to her surprise, without Bradley's assistance, Penelope quickly found the drawing room where the other guests were already assembled, awaiting the service of dinner. He had not given her a single hint.

To her even greater surprise, he had not tried to divert her to some secluded room. He had not even tried to touch her. Could there be hope for Bradley yet?

Candlelight shimmered across the fine china, glistened in the crystal goblets, and glinted over the fine silver. The highly polished depths of the dark mahogany furniture reflected the luminous candlelight. The fine Irish linens seemed to glow with a light of their own.

Penelope was dazzled by the soft radiance that enveloped the dining room. But when she took her seat with the others at the long table, she became completely bewildered.

She was used to drinking water, milk, or sometimes cider, from a plain earthenware cup. She had never been offered beverages like these—a wine the color of fluid garnets, or the strange straw-colored liquid that bubbled up from the bottom of the long, hollow-stemmed crystal goblet.

All her life, she had eaten from a single, battered pewter dish. The footman brought her a small white china bowl on a small white plate with gold garland edgings. The china was so fine that she could see the candlelight flickering through its opalescence as he placed both before her on another, larger, similarly decorated plate. Imagine anyone needing three plates for a simple bowl of soup! Small wonder she had been kept so busy at the stone sink in the scullery when working here.

In the sexton's cottage, a three-pronged tin fork had sufficed for bacon and potatoes, while a crudely made spoon was used for soup and porridge. In the kitchen, her mother had often used her one large knife—which never could keep an edge, no matter how many times they had the scissors grinder attend to it when he came to town. Never in her life had Penelope seen so many different shapes and sizes of utensils. She had no doubt that each had a specific purpose, none of which she knew!

She was used to sitting down to table with her father at one end and her mother at the end closest to the fire so she could tend to the meal. The last occasion Penelope had eaten with so many people was at last year's Michaelmas fair. Even then, they had all been outside, upon rugs on the grass, not seated at a table whose opposite end she could barely see!

Quickly she glanced at Corbett seated to her right. At least she had not been placed with someone she did not know, but with whom she would nevertheless have to converse politely. Still and all, she thought with a small grimace that she hurried to hide, she could have done without having Bradley seated to her left.

A footman held a large tureen from which another footman ladled a creamy brown soup into her bowl. How wonderfully delicious it smelled! She could see the mushrooms floating in the thick broth. She detected the scent of liver, but somehow it was more subtle than anything she was accustomed to. How hungry she was! And the aroma of this luscious soup only served to make her hungrier yet. Still, she was terrified to begin eating. She was quite certain that she would do something wrong.

Penelope stared, perplexed, at the puzzling display of knives, forks, and spoons, then glanced to her bowl of soup, then back again.

'Well, knives and forks are out of the question,' she reasoned. 'But which spoon?'

By the tiny taps of silver against china, Penelope could tell that the others had begun eating. How she longed to join them! But she was afraid to begin, afraid that everyone would see her ignorance.

Perhaps she could look to Corbett once again for assistance, she thought. He had been kind enough to have her released from jail. Of course, any fair-minded gentleman would have done the same thing, would he not? Would Corbett still be willing to help her? Or had he reverted to his old, haughty demeanor? Was he even now sitting there, watching her like the rest of them surely were, waiting to mock her slightest fault?

She dared to steal a quick glance at him. Much to her relief, he was not laughing at her. He was not even smiling. He was watching her intently. As she continued to meet his gaze, she could not help but notice the way he very carefully moved his hand over the array of silver until he stopped over a round-bowled spoon. He quite pointedly picked it up and began to eat.

Merciful heavens! Had he been watching her, waiting all this time just to show her the appropriate utensil? 'Twas exceedingly kind of him, no doubt. Penelope smiled and picked up her identical spoon. To show just how grateful she was for his assistance, she began eating her soup immediately.

"Quite delicious, isn't it?" Corbett asked.

Penelope stopped, the full spoon poised halfway to her mouth. She suddenly realized that she had been eating so quickly that she had actually barely tasted the soup.

"Yes, indeed," she answered, slowly lowering the spoon.

"I am rather fond of the Madeira in the soup," he said. "Although if one is not accustomed to it, one should consume only a small portion at a time—and then *very* slowly."

"Yes, I suppose that *is* wise," Penelope replied, grateful once again that Corbett had intervened when she was making a complete fool of herself.

More slowly, she dipped the bowl into the thick broth to scoop up a piece of mushroom. What she spooned up instead bore no resemblance to what she knew of the species. For a moment, she feared they had sent that shatter-brained maid, Pansy, out picking mushrooms. If that were the case, they would all be dead in the morning. While debating whether to eat the unidentified item or not, she merely sat there and frowned at it.

"How strange," Corbett whispered to her. "Your ravenous appetite has quickly disappeared after a few spoonfuls. Do you not like *foie gras*?"

Penelope's lips began to form the unfamiliar words, but never quite completed the task.

"Goose liver," Corbett explained in a whisper. "'Tis French. No need to concern yourself if you cannot pronounce the wretched tongue."

Penelope grinned and nodded her comprehension. She had identified the liver all by herself. Then she inclined her head toward her spoon. "But what is *that*?" she demanded of him under her breath.

"A truffle," he replied. When she still looked puzzled, he continued, "Rather like a fancy mushroom, which grows underground in the woods in the south of France. They use pigs to sniff them out and uproot them."

At this startling news, she dumped the contents of her spoon back into the bowl and began to refill her spoon with the broth and the other mushrooms, which she *knew* were safe to eat.

"They *are* edible, Lady Ermentrude," Corbett assured her. "Not to mention quite delicious."

Timidly, Penelope fished about in her broth until she had scooped up another piece of truffle. She ventured one more glance at Corbett—just to make certain he was not trying to tease her.

"If I am dead in the morning, 'twill be all your fault," she warned him.

Corbett laughed. "Eat your soup."

Penelope bravely swallowed her spoonful. She smiled. Corbett was correct.

"How are you finding your new accommodations in this lovely old manor?" Corbett asked.

"The house is very . . . big," she answered. "I believe my bedchamber alone is larger than our entire cottage."

"The Lords Bellingsford have played a role in the history of our country, a role in which you now have a part—and may I add, Lady Ermentrude, a very lovely part," Corbett said. "You must make certain that you have a grand tour of the manor."

"My dear little Penelope," Bradley suddenly interrupted, much to the shock and dismay of the abandoned lady seated to his other side. "I should be more than happy to conduct you on an extensive tour of the manor."

Penelope tried very hard to be polite and hide her annoyance at the interruption of her conversation with Corbett. "I doubt—" she began.

"Who better than myself could give you such an informed tour?" Bradley countered. "And who but myself would do it so willingly?"

"Oh, I daresay Lord Bellingsford would be most willing—even eager—to recount to his daughter all the family history," Corbett said. "I should say that *no one* would be better qualified than he."

Bradley glared at Corbett. "I should still be pleased to accompany you when Uncle Roger does conduct your tour, my dear little cousin," he said, leaning closer to her.

"We shall see," Penelope answered, unwilling to give assurances.

"Perhaps," Corbett suggested brightly, "Lord Bellingsford will conduct the entire house party upon that tour."

"My dear little cousin, a private tour is so much more informative," Bradley insisted.

She was extremely grateful for the footman who interposed himself between Bradley and her in order to remove her empty soup bowl, and for the other footmen, who brought around an amazing array of more delectable dishes to distract Bradley's attention from her. As each footman paused at her side, Penelope merely stared at the dish he proffered. Oh, how she wished Bradley would stop his insipid flatteries so she could concentrate on what Corbett was trying to show her.

"Do try some of the baked turbot, Lady Ermentrude," Corbett suggested. "Or perhaps the prawns."

The footman served her, then moved on, leaving her once again to ponder the intricacies of the silverware. Penelope turned immediately to Corbett, hoping again for his silent assistance. Again, he did not fail to indicate, silently, the proper tiny, two-pronged fork, nor to continue his amiable chatter so that no one would take undue notice of his attentions to her difficulties with the utensils.

''Tis hard to believe this is the same Corbett who so coldly left me four years ago,' Penelope thought with amazement. 'He is so polite, so kind now . . . now that I am . . .' her thoughts slowed and then froze in a heart-shattering stop as the dreadful realization came to her. 'Ever since he discovered that I am actually Lady Ermentrude Fairmount, only daughter and heiress of the very rich Roger Fairmount, Lord Bellingsford.'

Her stomach began to churn with the sudden turmoil of her feelings. She could almost believe that someone *had* put toadstools in her soup instead of mushrooms. The delicacies set before her lost all their exquisite flavors, turning heavy and sour in her mouth. No amount of water, or even the marvelous new taste of champagne, could banish the dryness in her throat.

Once again she had allowed Corbett Remington to hurt her! She was angry—as much with herself for her own gullibility as with Corbett for his callous opportunism.

'How *dare* he think me so easily fooled!' she silently fumed. 'The devil take that man! The devil take me too!' she added when she finally admitted to herself that she was, indeed, so easily duped. 'How could I have been so trusting? I should have known all along that he did not care for me. The haughty Corbett Remington could not stoop to love the lowly sexton's daughter, but only rise to court the daughter of an earl!'

To realize that Corbett had only been kind to her because he thought her worth a pound or two angered Penelope beyond words. The more she tried not to cry, the harder she clenched her teeth together. The harder she clenched her teeth together, the more she caused her head to ache.

At last, the interminable meal was finished. The gentlemen all rose as the ladies prepared to retire after dinner. Penelope was puzzled. After dinner at the sexton's cottage, she and her mother would clear away the food and dishes while her father, seated by the fire, smoked a single, daily pipe. Penelope believed she should rise with the rest of the ladies now, but the ache in her head and her continued bewilderment with the situation, not to mention her disillusionment with Corbett, left her unsure of precisely what to do.

Suddenly Corbett's hand was upon her elbow, assisting her to rise.

"Allow me, Lady Ermentrude. I know you are fairly exhausted after your long day," he said, raising his voice so it would carry even to the elderly ladies who glared at her censoriously from the far end of the table. "Perhaps you will feel more refreshed after you have retired."

"Oh, indeed," Margaret called to her from halfway down the table. She stretched out her hand and made her way to Penelope's side. "Come with me, Ermentrude. I have ever so much to tell you."

Gratefully, Penelope began to move away from the table.

Corbett's hand remained upon her arm. "I hope we may continue our conversation later," he said, smiling down upon her.

She could barely find the composure to answer him. "As the house party is to last a fortnight, I do not see how we shall be able to avoid it." She turned from him and left the room.

Corbett frowned with puzzlement as he watched her go. Indeed, there would be time—he would find it—he would *make* the time to talk to her about his true feelings for her. Still, 'twas a pity she felt so poorly this night, of all nights. Surely that was the cause of her sudden loss of appetite and her curt replies to him throughout the latter part of the meal after her previous warmth. He hoped she had not fallen ill due to some bad prawns.

When the gentlemen rejoined the ladies in the drawing room, Lord Bellingsford took Penelope's arm in his.

"Come, my dear," his lordship said. "I have been waiting for over twenty years to present you to these good people."

In spite of the furious ache in her head, not to mention the horrid ache in her heart caused by that horrid Corbett Remington, Penelope made the round of the drawing room. Somehow she managed to smile politely to each person there. Somehow she managed to answer their rather probing questions without making a raging fool of herself.

Somehow she managed to avoid Corbett, who was busily conversing with a group of people. She had already made the acquaintance of Miss Margaret Dilley, standing at Corbett's side. She quickly recognized the portly, balding gentleman to Margaret's other side as Lord Ormsley— although it was easy to see from his tall, lean figure that Corbett favored his late mother, Penelope decided. The two people standing to the other side of Corbett must be Margaret's parents. The physical resemblance was too marked for this not to be so.

Lord Bellingsford drew Penelope to a group of people who were standing behind Mr. and Mrs. Dilley. Penelope watched Mrs. Dilley glance to her right, then left, before speaking. She did not look to see Penelope behind her or else she surely would not have spoken so, Penelope believed—or would she?

"Well, there *is* a strong physical resemblance between them," Mrs. Dilley pointed out, taking great care that her voice carried to the edge of the circle. "No doubt she *is* Lord Bellingsford's daughter—regardless of which side of the blanket she was born, if you take my meaning."

Although he knew quite definitely what her meaning was, Corbett could not help but press the issue. "No, Mrs. Dilley. What *do* you mean?"

"Well, ah . . . at any rate . . . if you ask me . . ." She floundered until she recovered her original intention. "At any rate, I suppose it does not signify. If Lord Bellingsford wishes her to be his long-lost daughter, who am I to dispute it?" she asked, raising her hand, with great humility, to her bosom. "Still, 'tis easy enough to see she has not had a proper upbringing, as has my Margaret—who is not only beautiful, but highly accomplished as well."

Corbett merely nodded politely.

"Indeed, she is," Lord Ormsley agreed, appreciatively surveying the young lady he had specifically—and quite wisely, he believed—chosen as his son's future wife. He glared pointedly at his son, who was being most remiss in his duties as suitor to the lovely Miss Dilley. "How fortunate for the lucky man who captures such a prize!"

"But poor Lady Ermentrude has been raised, not as a proper lady, but with . . . you *did* say 'twas with the *gravedigger*—of all people—and his wife, did you not?" she demanded of Corbett.

"Mr. Graves is the sexton of the village church," Corbett offered quickly. "His wife is the vicar's housekeeper."

"Adequate people, I am sure," Mrs. Dilley said. "But, 'tis easy enough to see they are hardly the type to have raised a *lady*. One can tell that readily enough from Penelope's atrocious manners when eating!"

"How strange," Corbett remarked with exaggerated innocence. "I had thought her manners extraordinarily polished."

"Come now," Mrs. Dilley persisted. "She had not the least idea of the proper way to hold her knife or to peel off her prawns. Why, if it were not for you, Mr. Remington, I believe she would have eaten shells and all." She gave a snickering little laugh. "And did you see the look on her face when she first tasted the champagne?"

"I really doubt that prawns and champagne were frequently served at the church sexton's home," Corbett remarked acidly.

Mrs. Dilley pressed her lips together for a moment. Still, she could not be stopped. "Someone needs to take the girl in hand *immediately*," she pronounced with undisputed authority. "And she should not be released into polite society again until she has attained some social graces! The girl most certainly will do Lord Bellingsford no good the way she is now."

Upon first hearing Mrs. Dilley's scathing criticism, Penelope had wanted to turn her about and box the lady's ears smartly. How could such a carping, caviling woman have produced a daughter as kind and generous as Margaret? Penelope wondered. The more she heard of the lady's diatribe, the more she wanted only to leave the room, never to see that nasty person again.

But Lord Bellingsford still grasped Penelope's elbow firmly, and propelled her—horror of horrors!—in that lady's very direction. Penelope clenched her teeth more firmly together and steeled herself for the confrontation.

From behind Mrs. Dilley, Lord Bellingsford replied icily, "Merely finding her has done me good, madam."

The lady did not pause, nor even blush from embarrassment. She haughtily raised her chin. "Well, you must own, my lord, the girl *is* sorely lacking in social graces." She threw Penelope a withering glance.

"She will learn," Lord Bellingsford replied with great certainty. "Until such a time, if you find my daughter's social graces so annoying, madam, I am certain there are other houses where you can be better entertained."

"Oh, please understand, my lord," Mrs. Dilley said. Her eyes had suddenly grown ingenuously wide, and her voice became much less strident. "I am only telling you this for the girl's own good, of course."

"Of course," Lord Bellingsford replied. "How comforting to know my daughter's welfare is of such concern to you." Slowly, his lordship steered Penelope on to the next group of people.

Uncertain of how to address him now, Penelope whispered to Lord Bellingsford, "M'lord, please—"

"Can you not call me Father?" he asked.

Penelope nodded. Still, she found the word difficult to use. "If you please, I . . . I am so sorry to be an inconvenience, but . . . I have the most horrible headache. Might I retire?"

"Of course you must," Lord Bellingsford insisted, patting her hand solicitously. "I wouldn't want you to become ill— now that I've finally found you. You'll feel more like rejoining us in the morning after a good night's rest."

Penelope nodded her silent agreement and bade him good night. She did not tell him that no amount of rest would repair her aching heart.

She cautiously eyed Corbett as she left the room. Oh, how could a man with eyes like that make things so difficult for her?

Margaret placed her hand upon Lord Ormsley's arm and discreetly diverted his attention away from their own little group.

"Oh, pish tosh!" she complained in as much of a whisper as she was capable of producing. "Mama has been telling me that for as long as I can remember—and I do detest when she says it."

"Says what, Miss Dilley?" Lord Ormsley asked.

Margaret leaned closer to his lordship, so close, in fact, that the dark tresses piled atop her head fairly touched the remaining strands of graying brown hair at the sides of his.

In a conspiratorial whisper, she said, "There is absolutely *nothing* worse than when someone deliberately does something extraordinarily unpleasant—and then insists that they are only doing it for your own good!"

"Why, my dear Miss Dilley, not only are you extremely lovely," Lord Ormsley said with a deep chuckle, "you are also quite an astute young lady!"

CHAPTER
SEVEN

WAS PENELOPE'S ABILITY to find her way about Bellford
Manor improving, or had it merely taken some time for the
esoteric art of corridor navigation she supposed was imparted to a "ladyship" to take its effect on her? In spite of her
aching head, in almost no time at all she found her bedchamber. Grateful her search was at an end, she quickly opened
the door and sought refuge inside.

"You've retired early, *m'lady*," the maid said with what
Penelope could have sworn was a sneer.

"I . . . I am unwell," Penelope replied, reluctant to confide
her hurt to a stranger.

Not only was Penelope surprised to find someone in what
she had thought would be her own private sanctuary, she was
also extremely disappointed. All she wanted at the moment
was to be left alone with her headache and her misery. She
did not want to have to face yet another disparaging house
guest or taunting servant. Not tonight. Not now.

'I should have jumped from Lord Bellingsford's carriage
while I still had the opportunity,' she lamented, 'and run
back to the life I knew in my little cottage, the life I was sure
of.'

The dark-eyed maid was minutely scrutinizing some additional gowns and smallclothes that had been left upon the
bench at the foot of Penelope's bed. Languidly, she dropped
them back down and turned to face Penelope. She clucked
her tongue and shook her head. "Such a pity," she said with

what Penelope thought was a marked lack of sympathy. "Not used to all the finery, eh, *m'lady*?"

Penelope had no desire to acknowledge the impertinent maid's remark with a reply. Therefore, she merely eyed the girl disdainfully and said, "I suppose *you* are my new abigail." She fervently hoped she was not.

"I have that *honor*—for the time being," the maid replied. "Your ladyship can hire one of your own choice from London later, if you want."

'Just as soon as I am able,' Penelope silently decided. She was not completely familiar with a lady's requirements for her abigail, but she was more than a little suspicious that this girl did not meet them.

Penelope dug into her memory for a name to match with the narrow face and beady brown eyes that stared at her so coldly. "Gwenyth, isn't it?" she asked.

"Yes, 'tis, Lady Ermentrude."

'Oh, merciful heavens!' Penelope silently lamented. 'Even the scullery maids have prettier names than I!'

Gwenyth, indeed! Penelope fumed. They could not have sent a more incompetent person to be her lady's maid if they had sent up one of the stable boys.

From what she recalled of occasionally working with the girl in the kitchens, Penelope could just imagine Gwenyth returning below stairs, eager to relate in intimate detail each and every one of her new mistress's faults. Penelope could also easily envision the girl now throwing her elevated status of abigail up in the face of her former fellow scullery maids, and elbowing her way in amongst the other lady's maids who had truly worked to earn their deserved place in the hierarchy.

Gwenyth moved to stand behind Penelope. "I suppose your ladyship'll be wanting me to assist you out of that fine gown you *borrowed*."

Penelope was reluctant to accept Gwenyth's help. She most certainly did not want the girl seeing her in her old cotton small clothes. Still, she knew she would never be able to unfasten by herself all the tiny pearl buttons that ran up the back of Margaret Dilley's gown. And a true lady would *expect* her abigail to assist her, Penelope reasoned, would she not?

In order to uncover the buttons at the back of her dress, Gwenyth brushed Penelope's long tresses forward over her shoulder. They flipped into her face, causing Penelope to sputter and sneeze.

"Oh, begging your pardon, *m'lady*," the maid said.

Penelope was appalled at the manner in which the girl quickly unfastened the buttons, roughly pulled the pale blue silk gown over Penelope's head, and carelessly tossed it onto the bench. After all, 'twas a borrowed gown—all the more reason to give it extra care.

"Perhaps your ladyship should consider wrapping your hair back up into that knot like you used to," Gwenyth suggested, "instead of affecting styles what don't suit you at all."

Penelope was glad her back was to the impudent maid. Then she had enough time to compose herself before she coolly replied, "Perhaps a competent lady's maid could do something better with my hair—and my clothing. 'Tis evident *you* will never rise above the scullery, Gwenyth. I shall have to find another to wait on me tomorrow."

Gwenyth's silence told Penelope she had scored at least one point in this battle. Seizing her advantage, she ordered, "Now draw the curtains and retire," as she made her way to the large bed.

From whence came this newfound self-possession? Penelope wondered. Corbett had told her that she must learn to command the servants, but he had not told her how. Perhaps this new confidence was another benefit belatedly bestowed with the title. Suppressing an ill-timed giggle, Penelope thought she could hardly wait to see what endowment came next—although, if she had her choice, she did think having the ability to read other people's minds might prove extremely useful.

Penelope lifted above her head the soft, delicately embroidered night rail that lay across the foot of her bed. Nothing else she had ever worn smoothed down over her skin like this exquisite garment. Judging from the quality of the night rail, and the rest of the clothing on the bench, not to mention the temperament of those she had met here at Bellford Manor, she supposed they were all another loan from Miss Dilley. She must remember to thank Margaret tomorrow for her generosity.

"I shan't be needing your services the remainder of the evening, Gwenyth," Penelope told her. She was not ordinarily a spiteful person, but she could not resist adding, "But stay at hand—just in case I do." That should keep the tart-tongued wench from slipping off yet again into the woods with a footman—at least for tonight.

Penelope eased herself onto the soft feather mattress. Much to her surprise and relief, Gwenyth did indeed pull the long gold damask window draperies closed. Penelope was grateful for the darkness. Then she heard her close the door that connected her bedchamber to the maid's smaller, adjoining one. Penelope pulled her bed curtain closed and settled down to try to fall asleep.

She lay enfolded in the fine linen sheets covering the soft down-filled mattress. 'Twas smooth and fine, not as lumpy as her goose-feather mattress at home. Still, 'twas not *her* mattress. It lacked the comfort of the little hollows and rises that molded to her body in her own bed in the little room that had been added to the side of the cottage when she was small. No matter how she twisted and turned, Penelope could not get comfortable enough to fall asleep.

Her head still ached terribly. Her eyes refused to stay closed. She stared, wide-eyed, into the darkness, listening to all the sounds the large old house made, sounds to which she was completely unaccustomed.

She listened to the small gold and enamel clock on the carved marble mantelpiece ticking away the interminable seconds of the night. She heard the last log crumble to ashes as it burned itself out in the embers. She could hear the distant sounds of laughter, and the stairs creaking, and doors opening and closing as Lord Bellingsford's house guests retired to their respective bedchambers.

'It must be near dawn,' Penelope decided, recalling the late hour at which Lord Bellingsford's guests usually retired. 'I would wager Mr. Corbett Remington is having no such difficulties falling asleep,' she thought rather uncharitably as she continued to flounder against the pillows.

She could bear her sleeplessness no longer. Penelope sat upright in the bed. She pulled aside the bed curtain at her head. The weak glow peeking through the draperies confirmed her supposition. 'Twas not quite dawn.

She rose and, in the half-light, made her way slowly across the room to the window. She drew back one panel and looked out. My gracious! Even the attic story of the inn had not been this high! She fancied she should see clouds floating by.

Quickly she ducked back, afraid that she would fall out the window to plummet to her death on the pavement so far below. Still clutching the drapery, she looked out across the countryside, taking great care not to look down again. The carefully clipped lawns sloped toward the parkland and a small copse beyond that. Above the russet and gold treetops, Penelope could see the spire of her own little church silhouetted in the light of the rising sun. She knew that merely another field's length beyond there lay her parents' cottage.

Knowing that the two people who had loved and cared for her as a child, and who still loved and cared for her, were almost within sight, Penelope did not feel quite so alone in this strange new place. She thought of Margaret Dilley, a rather peculiar character, but a friend, nonetheless. She thought of Corbett, the only man she had ever loved, still so far from ever being her own—and yet closer now somehow. She felt the tightness draining from her shoulders and the back of her neck. Her headache began to lessen. A bit more relieved, Penelope stumbled back to the comfort that her bed finally afforded her. At long last, she fell into a dreamless sleep.

"Come, come, m'lady," the cheerful voice shocked her awake. The gold draperies were ripped back, allowing the bright morning light to flood her room.

It could not possibly be Gwenyth who was so perky—unless she were doing this for revenge, Penelope thought as she pulled the covers over her head in an attempt to shut out the noise.

"Go away, Gwenyth," Penelope ordered. " 'Tis much too early to be rising." Especially since she had fallen asleep barely an hour ago.

"No, silly, 'tis I," Margaret said as she pulled back the bedcurtains.

Penelope slowly lowered the covers. Margaret's smiling face peered down at her.

"Come now, do not be a slugabed!" Margaret ordered. "We are going riding and you must join us."

"I *must*?" Penelope repeated. She tried to use a tone of voice which could in no way whatsoever be mistaken for the slightest bit of enthusiasm.

"Lord Bellingsford said 'twill not be a party without you," Margaret told her with a cheery grin. She reached out for Penelope's hand to coax her from the bed.

Penelope heaved a weary sigh. She would not want to disappoint Lord Bellingsford. She felt guilty enough for any embarrassment her early departure from the dinner party last night might have caused him. Slowly, and very reluctantly, she dragged her limp body from the warm—and suddenly much more comfortable—bed.

"What happened to Gwenyth?" she asked. Of course, Gwenyth could be on her way to Timbuktu and she really would not give a fig. On the other hand, at this hour of the morning, there was something to be said for a sullen, silent abigail. The last time she had heard anything as loud as Margaret at such an early hour of the morning was the past autumn when they had slaughtered the hogs at Dan Wilkins' farm.

Margaret waved her hand through the air as if that would cause Gwenyth to disappear completely. "Oh, I told her you said you would not be requiring her services this morning."

Penelope was shocked by Margaret's boldness. On the other hand, she was rather glad to be rid of Gwenyth—even if only temporarily.

"Oh, she fretted and pouted and pleaded with me not to make her lose her situation. But I told her I could take care of you far better than she can. And I shall," Margaret reassured her. "Oh, I am having ever so much fun doing this! I do hope you are, too, Penelope."

Penelope looked about her. Margaret's abigail had carried a small silver tray into the room and placed it on the table beside Penelope's bed. She lifted the small pot and poured a cup of chocolate. Penelope chose one of the hot scones from the plate on the tray and bit into the buttery softness, then took a sip of the warm chocolate. When she looked at the eager smile on Margaret's rounded face, Penelope decided that, indeed, she was having fun.

Penelope's heart lurched when Margaret picked up the blue silk gown and carelessly tossed it to her abigail, who deftly caught it and immediately took it from the room.

"I see you found my night rail. Did you get to try any of the other things?" Margaret asked.

"I did not have the opportunity last night," Penelope admitted. She rose from the bed and donned the dressing gown that Margaret handed her.

"I suppose not. You did look rather piqued, and not in any condition to pretend to be at the modiste's." Margaret grinned at her. "At any rate, it does not signify," she added when her abigail returned carrying several riding habits of varying hues over her arm. "Now, I have the loveliest riding habit—a deep green, which should suit your coloration just perfectly—and 'tis a bit too snug on me, so . . ."

Penelope began to believe that Margaret could say the same for almost all her clothing.

"There is a brown one, too, but I do not think that color would suit you as well." Margaret seized her hand and pulled her enthusiastically toward the stack of new clothing.

"But, Margaret, I cannot go riding," Penelope interrupted, resisting Margaret's compelling tug. "I do not know how."

Margaret appeared to be quite surprised by this startling revelation. "You do not know how to ride? But . . . but I thought every country miss knew how to ride."

"We never owned any animals. Oh, well, we do have our chickens," Penelope admitted. "But nothing so large as a horse. Horses are far too expensive for people like us to keep."

"Well, fancy that! At any rate, that does not signify either. You must choose one of these and wear it," Margaret insisted. She began to sort through the outfits that the abigail had draped over the chairs for Penelope's perusal. " 'Tis a shame, you know, to allow such lovely things to go to waste simply because one cannot ride. Do you think *I* can ride?"

Penelope nodded. "Well, yes, I rather thought you did, especially since you own all these," she said, gesturing to the riding habits.

Margaret gave a hearty laugh. "Well, I can sit a horse well enough not to fall off when the beast begins to move," she modestly admitted. "But I do not actually *ride*. Mama insisted upon buying all these, regardless, so I wear them to sit in the saddle and look pretty. You, too, can do just that, Penelope," she reassured her with a laugh. "With a little practice, probably even as well as I can."

The ladies watched with coldly assessing looks as the groom led Penelope's gentle little brown mare into the large stableyard. Margaret smiled her encouragement. Lord Bellingsford's eyes were bright with pride. The other gentlemen stared with undisguised admiration.

Penelope looked for Corbett in the throng. At last she saw

him at the edge of the crowd. He was smiling at her, as if he were delighted to see her atop this beast.

'If only he could know how miserable I truly am,' Penelope thought. Her right leg already ached from trying to grip the horn of the sidesaddle so she would not go sliding off. Her fingers hurt from clinging to the reins and the pommel of the saddle. Her mouth and throat were dry with fear.

Thank heavens the grooms had assisted her to mount while she was still in the stables. At least everyone had not witnessed her awkward first attempts at sitting a horse. Thank heavens the horse, Merriweather, was a placid little thing.

Mrs. Dilley glared at Penelope. Why did the girl have to wear her long blonde hair plaited and wound about her head like some sort of coronet or, worse yet, a halo, beneath the brim of her fetching green hat? Must her skin have the look of porcelain in the early morning sunlight? Did her pale green eyes have to look so wide with fear and bewilderment?

Mrs. Dilley pursed her lips as she observed the reactions of each of the gentlemen seated on their respective mounts, and even of the grooms and stable boys standing about the yard. Each and every one of the fools looked more than willing to lay down his life to protect the blasted chit should the horse prove intractable!

Why did the girl's figure have to look so lovely in that deep green riding habit—*Margaret*'s riding habit? How could her own daughter be so stupid as to assist the competition? Mrs. Dilley pondered with dismay. Oh, where had she gone wrong in raising the child? Could Margaret not see, the way Mrs. Dilley so easily could, that Corbett was more than a little taken with this Penelope, or Ermentrude, or whoever she was today? Did her foolish daughter not even care about how hard her mother had worked to get her a prospective viscount?

'Twas common knowledge that the Remingtons had once lived in this area of the county. Mrs. Dilley had suspected from the first, by the very manner in which Corbett had sprung from his chair at the breakfast table to rescue the girl from jail, that, obviously, there was a connection here that went back farther than one would at first suppose from their disparate stations in life.

She threw a quick glance in Lord Ormsley's direction. Why was he so busy conversing with Margaret when he should be whipping that recalcitrant son of his to come up to the mark and do the pretty? Lord Ormsley, Mr. Dilley, and she had agreed months ago to betroth Margaret and Corbett. They had almost succeeded in convincing Margaret and Corbett of the wisdom of their choice.

'The last thing I need at this moment is to have Penelope, or Ermentrude, or whoever this little upstart is, attracting Corbett's attention away from Margaret,' Mrs. Dilley silently fumed.

She pressed her wrinkled lips together tightly and frowned into the sunlight. She determined to do whatever was necessary to keep those two apart.

"Lady Ermentrude," Mrs. Dilley called, drawing her mount so close that the little brown mare shied and sidestepped, almost dislodging Penelope from her precarious perch. "How charming you look in Margaret's riding habit! Does she not, Mr. Remington?" Without waiting for him to reply, she added, "And was it not kind of Margaret to lend it to her?"

Penelope merely nodded. She was far too preoccupied with keeping the lovely riding habit—and herself inside it—up on the horse and out of the dirt of the stableyard floor, to have to worry about responding to Mrs. Dilley.

"How brave of you to be out riding so early this morning. Why, one could scarcely guess you were so ill last night," Mrs. Dilley continued. "Was it the prawns, Lady Ermentrude? Are you quite certain you should be up and about this morning?"

"No, they were quite fine," Penelope answered. " 'Twas simply the excitement of the evening, I suppose. And please, madam, could you call me Penelope?"

"But, my dear," Mrs. Dilley protested, "I had thought you would be proud to be called Lady Ermentrude. I suppose I was wrong," she added with a sigh. "How disappointed your father will be to hear of this."

"No, no," Penelope said. " 'Tis just that I am accustomed to being called—"

"Well, you will simply have to become accustomed to being called Ermentrude, won't you?" Mrs. Dilley reminded her with a persuasive pat on the hand with her riding crop. "After all, it is who you are now, with all the privileges and advantages—not to mention the responsibilities—that attend that name." Mrs. Dilley reached out to run her fingers over the fine wool of the riding habit. "After all, I seriously doubt that you would be willing to return to your former name and your former lowly estate, would you?"

"My dear little cousin will never be considered lowly again," Bradley said as he drew his horse up to Penelope's other side.

Poor Merriwether sidestepped uneasily, yet, stuck between Bradley and Mrs. Dilley, she truly had no room to move.

"But you do look rather ill at ease atop Merriwether," Bradley commented. "I had thought she rather suited you, but if she does not . . . well, I can always order you another mount."

Penelope glanced down at Merriwether, the little brown mare again becoming more calm. Another mount might not prove quite so amenable, she feared. And even if it did, changing horses would entail repeating the entire process of getting up into the saddle.

"I believe I shall stay with Merriwether," she decided. Tentatively, she released the reins with one hand and reached out to pat the mare's soft brown neck. Actually, she thought she was being extraordinarily brave in accomplishing this feat.

Merriwether snorted and shook her head, sending her

mane tossing back and forth. Penelope quickly drew back her hand, clutching the reins even more tightly.

"Come now," Lord Bellingsford called to his guests. "Let us begone from here. The morning passes and the countryside awaits."

The clatter of hooves on the cobblestones filled the stableyard as the house guests urged their horses into a trot.

After most of the other guests had eagerly left the stableyard, Lord Ormsley joined Margaret as they allowed their horses merely to walk side by side through the large wooden gate.

"Do you enjoy riding, Miss Dilley?" Lord Ormsley asked.

"Not particularly," Margaret admitted.

Lord Ormsley turned to her and, almost as if inquiring after a confidence, whispered, "What do you dislike most about it?"

"Aside from the odor?"

"We shall take that as a given," Lord Ormsley conceded with a nod.

"In that case, I should say that I can think of any number of things that I would rather be doing."

"Such as?"

"Oh, dancing, shopping—while standing up," she qualified her statement.

"And what do you enjoy while sitting down?"

"Oh, sometimes playing cards—or eating, indubitably," Margaret declared emphatically.

Lord Ormsley laughed. "I am quite in agreement with you."

"But, my lord, I thought all gentlemen enjoyed riding!" Margaret declared with surprise. "Might I inquire why a robust gentleman such as yourself would dislike riding?"

"Oh, I am far too old for such foolishness," he admitted. A blush suffused his cheeks.

"Stuff and nonsense, my lord!" Margaret declared stoutly. "I find it quite impossible to consider *you* too old for any kind of foolishness."

Lord Ormsley's blush continued to spread to the very top of his head.

Penelope wisely held back until everyone else had left the stableyard. With Mrs. Dilley on one side of her and Bradley on the other, it was difficult for anyone else to draw nearer to her. Still, Penelope noted that Corbett tried to stay close by.

"Do you need assistance, Lady Ermentrude?" Corbett offered.

Penelope turned from watching, rather enviously, the other ladies as they trotted their horses merrily, and quite competently, from the stableyard. She watched Corbett for a second or two, trying to decide precisely what to say before she actually answered him. True, he had been very helpful to her throughout the entire ordeal yesterday. But when she recalled that he was only being considerate of her because she was now worth several tens of thousands of pounds a year, she was rather reluctant to accept anything from him.

Before she could respond, Bradley took hold of the reins of her horse and began to lead her from the stableyard. "My cousin needs no assistance from strangers, Mr. Remington," Bradley said. "We Fairmounts can take care of our own."

Mrs. Dilley quickly turned to Corbett and said, "Come, Mr. Remington. You and I will find Margaret."

Was Merriwether unhappy being led out of the stableyard by Bradley? Was Mrs. Dilley's horse following Merriwether much too closely for her comfort? Should they cast the blame upon some passing bee, or was Merriwether simply not the gentle mare they all mistook her for? Something was to blame for the way the little brown mare suddenly kicked up her heels, took off at a wild gallop across the pasture, leaped the fence, and headed over the fields with Penelope clinging desperately to her mane.

CHAPTER
EIGHT

THE LITTLE MARE carried her past the group of riders so quickly that Penelope barely heard their shouts. "Tallyho! Halloo!" some of the more frivolous riders bellowed. "Oh, my God! Ermentrude! My daughter!" she heard Lord Bellingsford cry out.

She knew that some of them were coming after her. She also knew, as surely as if she could read that blasted horse's mind, that Merriwether had no intention of allowing them to catch her.

Penelope pulled at the reins until her arms and fingers ached, but Merriwether continued her headlong plunge over the countryside. Oh, why could she not command this animal as easily as she had commanded Gwenyth? The animal wasn't that much more intelligent.

"I shall see you in the mine pits, you flea-bitten bag of bones! I shall see you in the glue pot—and take great personal pleasure in keeping a pot of you upon my very own desk!" she furiously threatened the runaway horse—all to no avail. The wind whipped her words back into her face. At any rate, Penelope seriously doubted that the horse was listening to her. Merriwether had a destination of her own firmly in mind and would not be swayed.

Would the horror of this ride only end when Penelope had fallen to the ground and broken her neck? As if she did not have enough to worry about, the awful thought dawned upon her—would they inscribe 'Penelope' or 'Ermentrude' on her tombstone? Since Lord Bellingsford would be paying for it, she supposed she would be stuck with 'Ermentrude' for all eternity. This disheartening thought gave Penelope all the more reason to want to live. She clung even more tightly to the mare's thick mane as they headed across the lawn and into the small copse.

One by one, her would-be rescuers had abandoned the chase. From behind, Penelope could hear a lone horseman still pursue her. The dense undergrowth of the copse had forced Merriwether to slow a bit, but she had not yet seen fit to stop her precipitous journey. Nor could the rescuers catch and stop the wretched beast.

The copse opened suddenly into a small clearing. Merriwether stopped and lowered her head so abruptly that Penelope, still clutching her mane, went tumbling headlong off the horse and onto the soft carpet of grass below.

Too dizzy to move, Penelope lay flat upon her back, staring up into the sky until the world should cease its mad spinning.

Merriwether snorted and shied away when the rider burst into the clearing.

"Penelope! You cannot be dead!" Corbett cried as he jumped from his horse and fell to his knees by her side. Carefully cradling her head, he gently lifted her into his arms.

In a voice barely above a whisper, she managed to plead, "Just do not let them inscribe 'Ermentrude.' "

"You have struck your head." Corbett removed her hat and began to run his fingers gently over her head, searching for an injury, but the corona of her thick blonde braid kept interfering with the proper examination. Was it a lump or merely a piece of her hair?

"Oh, do stop," she ordered, slapping his hand away. "I look wretched enough already. No need for you to muss my hair further."

With a small chuckle, Corbett ceased his examination and cradled her more closely in his arms. "I suppose you *are* well enough if you are so concerned for your coiffure. Did you enjoy your jaunty little ride, my lady?"

"Jaunty little ride!" she cried indignantly. Abruptly, she pulled herself upright and pointed toward the offensive animal, now grazing contentedly at the far end of the clearing. "If I had a pistol, I would shoot that blasted horse where she stands!"

"I would not lay all the blame at poor Merriwether's feet—or rather, hooves," he said.

Frowning with puzzlement, she looked up at him. "What do you mean?"

Corbett shook his head. "Nothing. 'Twas nothing," he reassured her. "Apparently poor little Merriwether is strictly a children's mount—"

"Then why on earth did they give her to me?" she demanded. "*Who* would have given her to me? Surely not Lord Bellingsford!"

"Surely not," Corbett agreed. He was not certain why anyone would, but already he had determined to find out. "Merriwether could not deal with the excitement generated by all the other horses and riders there this morning."

"She could not bear Mrs. Dilley's crowding?" Penelope offered.

Without any evidence, Corbett was unwilling to fix the blame definitely in Penelope's mind and make her all the more uneasy at Bellford Manor. She was having enough trouble already. He shrugged and continued, "Or Bradley's lead, or fluttering leaves, or even the flapping skirts of the riding habits."

"Riding habit!" Penelope exclaimed. ''Oh, merciful heavens, I hope I have not ruined it." She attempted to scramble to her feet without doing further damage to the borrowed habit.

"Allow me to assist you," Corbett said, extending his hand to her. Once she was steady upon her feet, he drew her close to him. "Are you certain you have injured nothing?"

"Only my pride," she answered. "To tell the truth, I do not

feel as bad as I had thought I would. Of course, I had thought I would be dead, so I suppose anything is an improvement."

Corbett chuckled and pulled her so close to him that he could feel her heart still pounding madly in her chest, and her breasts rising and falling as she took deep breaths of air.

He, too, had feared he would find only her broken, lifeless body. Slowly, he enveloped her in his embrace. How much better to be holding the warm, breathing woman in his arms. He brought his hand up to her chin, and traced the soft pink outline of her lips with his finger. He lifted her face to his. Within a matter of mere seconds, he would place his lips upon hers.

Merriwether snorted and pranced about the clearing. Penelope heard the sound of another horse approaching them through the woods. Quickly she pulled away from Corbett's arms and began brushing the dirt and leaves and blades of grass from her skirt. Corbett moved off in pursuit of Merriwether.

"Ah, my dear little cousin!" Bradley exclaimed as his horse burst into the clearing. "I am so glad to find you. Uncle Roger will be quite relieved that you are safe."

"Doubtless everyone else will, too," Corbett remarked from across the clearing.

"Doubtless," Bradley agreed. "Come, Penelope. I shall take you home so you may rest"—he shot Corbett a condescending glare—"while Mr. Remington kindly sees to the horses."

Apparently, Corbett had been examining the saddle and accoutrements before he brought the recalcitrant Merriwether to Penelope's side. Penelope moved cautiously away. Never again did she want to have anything to do with any horse in general—and that wretched horse in particular!

"I am afraid not, Bradley," Corbett said. "Lady Ermentrude was just telling me how she completely agreed with the theory that in order to learn to ride properly, if one is thrown from a horse, one must immediately remount."

"Indeed, Mr. Remington?" Bradley said skeptically.

"Indeed, Mr. Remington," Penelope repeated, with much the same lack of charity that she felt toward Merriwether at this moment.

Before she could protest further, Corbett seized her about the waist and easily lifted her to sit upon his own well-trained mount.

"Not so terrible now, is it?" Corbett asked—and gave her a most impertinent wink!

"I can think of other things much worse," Penelope said, glaring at him. She decided to wait until a later time to enumerate these things to Corbett, and to make certain that he knew she wished each and every one of them to happen to him—and the wretched horse who trailed behind.

Corbett swung himself up into the saddle behind her. "As you can plainly see, I have everything well in hand here, Bradley. Why do you not ride ahead," he suggested, "and inform everyone that Lady Ermentrude is well?"

Corbett watched Bradley's consternation with amusement and just a bit of smug satisfaction. Bradley could hardly wrestle Penelope from his custody without causing undue fuss. Corbett would be taking Penelope home.

"I shan't be far ahead, Penelope," Bradley said.

As if that were supposed to reassure her! Penelope thought.

Bradley turned his mount and proceeded into the woods to return to Bellford Manor ahead of them.

Corbett took Merriwether by the reins. He guided his own horse slowly about the clearing, making certain that Merriwether was well under his control before leading her through the woods toward Bellford Manor.

Feeling the strength and warmth of Corbett's arms about her, Penelope could almost forgive him for again placing her atop this beast. 'Twas not an unpleasant feeling, leaning upon Corbett. Still, Penelope felt extraordinarily uncomfortable where she was.

"So now that I am back up upon this wretched nag," Penelope said, "do you think 'twill make me a better equestrienne?"

Corbett nodded and shifted her weight so that she rested more closely against his chest. "Doubtless."

"No, I never want to ride again, Corbett," she told him earnestly. "Not for as long as I live."

"Yes, you will," he answered confidently.

"Oh, no," she insisted. "I shall ask Lord Bellingsford to order me a fine phaeton, and hire a coachman, and a footman—or two—and I shall never have to go anywhere on horseback."

Corbett chuckled at her grand scheme. "You *shall* learn to ride," he insisted.

"How can you be so certain of what I will or will not do?" she demanded testily.

"Because Lord Bellingsford expects you to ride again," he told her. "His lordship has been so kind to you, Penelope. He would be very disappointed never to see you on horseback again."

Penelope nodded her agreement. Then she remembered her fearful ride and shrugged. "I think I shall be able to live with my guilt."

Then, in a conspiratorial whisper, Corbett reminded her, "And Mrs. Dilley expects you not to."

"If I allow Mrs. Dilley to be proven correct in this," she mused, almost as if she were thinking aloud, "I should never be able to look at myself in the mirror again!"

Penelope turned back to him as far as the close confines of the saddle would allow. Corbett gave her a triumphant grin.

"You are quite persuasive, sir," she conceded at last. "I marvel that you do not run for Parliament."

"Ah, but if I won, then I should never be able to go to London again, until I had been unseated," Corbett replied with an exaggerated sigh, "for fear that I should actually be made to do my job."

Even after her frightening ordeal, hearing Corbett laugh and jest again made Penelope begin to relax. She closed her eyes and snuggled up against the comfort of his broad chest. For a little while—only as long as it took them to ride back to Bellford Manor—she could pretend she was still just plain Penelope Graves again and that the Corbett Remington she knew and loved had returned.

Dinner was not quite so difficult to eat this evening. In fact, Penelope thought she should have enjoyed herself immensely were it not for two small problems. Taking advantage of Lord Bellingsford's customary lack of formal seating at his house parties, Mrs. Dilley had seized Corbett tonight, and hauled him off to the far end of the table, to sit between herself and her daughter, while Bradley remained at Penelope's side. To make matters worse, the longer she sat at the table, the more Penelope could feel the muscles of her legs tightening into painful knots.

"You look ill at ease, dear little cousin," Bradley said. "I feared as much from your horrendous experience upon Merriwether. Allow me to assist you."

He moved her water goblet and wineglasses closer within her reach. He assisted her with each choice of dishes offered.

'He has done everything but cut my meat and chew it for me!' Penelope wailed. 'Twas easy enough to dislike Bradley when he was a lecherous drunk. Yet he was no longer drunk and he had not touched her all evening. He had not even said anything which might be misconstrued as lewd. How could she dislike him now simply because he was too nice? Somehow, she was not surprised to find that she did not need a reason to dislike him. She longed for the dinner to end.

As the ladies prepared to retire, Lord Bellingsford rose and tapped his wineglass. "Gentlemen, might I suggest that we not dawdle overlong at our port," his lordship said. "I understand that this evening the ladies have prepared a delightful musical entertainment for us. Is that not so?" He directed his question at Mrs. Dilley, leaving no doubt in Penelope's mind whatsoever who was responsible for this—and who the premiere pianist would be.

Still and all, Penelope did enjoy listening to music. She wondered how well Margaret could play. The organist's preludes and postludes were always her favorite part of the church service—although if the Reverend Mr. Wroxley had asked, she would have pronounced his inspiring sermons to be her favorite.

She winced as she rose from the dining room chair—one more reason to curse that blasted Merriwether.

"You must allow me to assist you," Bradley insisted.

Given the choice between accepting Bradley's proffered arm or hobbling about like a gout-stricken debauchee, Penelope chose Bradley. And, if the truth be owned, he *was* much more tolerable than he used to be.

Much to her surprise, as Penelope limped into the music room supported by Bradley, Margaret was not the person seated at the large rosewood piano. In fact, Penelope was beginning to wonder when Margaret would play. One after the other, each young lady did her best, with varying degrees of success, to impress the assembled, eligible gentlemen with her performance.

Just when Penelope thought she would burst with anticipation, Mrs. Dilley at last drew Margaret to the piano. Then, waving furiously, she summoned Penelope to her side upon a small sofa directly behind Margaret and facing the other guests. Penelope expected Mrs. Dilley to have some pressing business or piece of news to impart, but the lady merely sat there beside her, listening to the music.

Margaret played a very intricate piece quite well. Upon its completion, she immediately began another, playing it with equal skill. Penelope was enchanted with the lovely sounds that Margaret was able to coax from the slim ebony and ivory keys.

"I believe I liked the Bach better," Mrs. Dilley whispered to Penelope. "Didn't you?"

Penelope nodded silently, not wishing to miss a single note of Margaret's wonderful performance. 'Twas rather rude of Mrs. Dilley to try to converse while Margaret, her very own daughter, was performing.

"Then again, there was the Mozart prelude," Mrs. Dilley said.

Not knowing the difference between any of the pieces, Penelope answered, "They are all nice."

"What will you play, Lady Ermentrude?"

"Oh, no. Nothing," Penelope answered, quite flustered that anyone would assume that she knew how to play.

"What was that you said?" Mrs. Dilley demanded, turning her ear in Penelope's direction. "I am afraid I am rather hard of hearing."

Penelope could not recall Mrs. Dilley suffering from that malady previously. Nevertheless, she leaned closer to the lady and repeated, "I shan't be playing."

"Well, why ever not?" Mrs. Dilley exclaimed. "You are among friends. No need to be shy, my dear. Play something," she urged.

"But, I cannot play," Penelope reluctantly admitted in a whisper so as not to disturb Margaret's performance.

"I beg your pardon," Mrs. Dilley said while tapping her foot in time to the music. "What did you say?"

Penelope raised her voice only slightly. "I cannot play."

Mrs. Dilley was still quite deliberately tapping her foot to Margaret's crescendoing chords. "Oh dear, this is the loudest part. Could you please repeat for my poor old ears what you just said?"

Penelope was becoming increasingly irritated. 'If you were paying attention to what I was saying instead of concentrating on tapping your foot, you could hear me,' she thought with disgust.

Drowned out by the loud music, Penelope believed she should be able to raise her voice enough for Mrs. Dilley to hear her. Penelope took a deep breath and shouted, "I do not know how to play!" immediately after Margaret's music came to a crashing finale.

All eyes focused on Penelope. Everyone in the room had

heard her. Mrs. Dilley smiled with satisfaction. She had timed that just perfectly!

"Oh, dear," a lady in the back murmured. "The chit has no social graces, no graces at all!" From about the room, small titters began to circulate, growing until someone laughed aloud and the rest joined in.

That was the outside of enough! Penelope held her breath so her nose would not run, and tried to hold back her tears.

'I shan't have them see me cry!' she promised herself.

In spite of the overwhelming urge to run from the room, Penelope rose calmly from the sofa. She made her way slowly to Lord Bellingsford, dropped him a short curtsey, then left the room. 'Twas not until she heard the door close firmly behind her that she began to run. 'Twas not bad enough that, once again, she had succeeded in making a complete fool of herself! She had allowed Mrs. Dilley to make a fool of her! She did not know, nor did she care, where she was going in the big house, just as long as she was away from everyone there who would ridicule her.

"I must see to my daughter," Lord Bellingsford insisted, heading for the door through which Penelope had just fled. "She must be made to realize, surely, they meant no harm."

"Surely not, my lord," Mrs. Dilley agreed. "But you really must not leave your guests."

Corbett readily volunteered, "I shall find her, my lord."

"She will be much more comforted by a member of her own family," Bradley interjected.

"You will miss all the lovely music, Mr. Remington," Mrs. Dilley added. "Margaret still has several pieces—"

"With your permission, my lord," Corbett said, although he really did not wait for his lordship's response before he left the room. He knew his departure from Mrs. Dilley bordered on rude, but . . . oh, what the deuce! 'Twas more important to him to find Penelope!

Mrs. Dilley pursed her lips with disgust. How in heaven's name was she going to accomplish this alliance if Corbett continued to run so shamelessly after that little upstart? How dare Lord Bellingsford be so extremely rude as to time the finding of his long-lost daughter so badly—just when she was about to finally ensnare Corbett Remington for *her* daughter!

Still and all, it did not really seem to make much difference if he went or he stayed, as Corbett did not pay much attention to Margaret or her wonderful performance.

Ah well, it did not signify, Mrs. Dilley thought philosophically. Lord Ormsley appeared to be *quite* impressed with Margaret's musical ability.

After all the confusion, the formal musicale appeared to have disbanded. Guests were sitting or standing about in little groups, gossiping. Lord Ormsley had moved to the piano and was helping Margaret to choose her next selection. Heavens above! He was even singing with her—and everyone was listening! Oh, how could anyone appreciate Margaret's clear, lovely soprano with Lord Ormsley growling away in his exceptionally loud, and just slightly off-key, bass? Much to Mrs. Dilley's astonishment, however, Margaret, in spite of her finely trained ear, did not seem to mind his lordship's caterwauling in the least. Why, the girl was actually encouraging his lordship's participation. Mrs. Dilley watched with growing satisfaction. Perhaps Margaret was not so shatter-brained after all. At least she had enough sense to try to charm her future father-in-law.

Mrs. Dilley nodded her approval. She was quite reassured that, at the proper time, Lord Ormsley would insist upon his son making Margaret an honorable offer—but, things being what they were right now, it had best be soon.

Once again, Penelope had succeeded in getting herself lost. Where had she gone wrong? She had found her bedchamber so easily before. Where was it now? Had she lost her ability to navigate these corridors? Was this fate's way of telling her she truly was not a lady after all and had no business whatsoever being here?

She was so near to tears already, the futility of her search was drawing them closer to the surface. She gave up the quest in a vacant sitting room, illuminated by a single candle. She sat on a small sofa tucked away in a window alcove. Alone, she allowed the tears to flow.

She heard the footsteps at the far end of the sitting room and someone calling her name. She stifled her noisy sobs, drew her feet up onto the seat, and pushed herself back into the cushions, as if she could blend into the upholstery and make herself invisible. The mysterious footsteps drew closer until they stopped in front of her. She did not look up. She hoped it was true what little children believed—if she could not see him, he could not see her.

"Penelope!" Corbett exclaimed.

"Oh, drat! It does not work," she mumbled. She slumped against the cushions with disappointment.

"What does not work? Penelope, are you quite certain you did not hit your head when you fell from the horse?" Corbett demanded.

"It does not signify," she answered as she untangled her feet from beneath her and sat upright upon the sofa. She rubbed her hands over her eyes to wipe away the tears. She sniffed loudly.

Seating himself beside her, Corbett offered her a large silk handkerchief.

After she had dried her eyes, she turned to him and asked, "Tell me, Corbett, why do you call me Penelope now that we are alone, but insist upon calling me by that other horrid name whenever the others are around?"

"Because *I* already know who you are, Penelope," he answered. "But there must be no mistaking on the part of the others as to who you *truly* are."

"Is it that important that I be Lady Ermentrude?"

Corbett shrugged. "It is to Lord Bellingsford."

Penelope looked up at him. "And to you," she added.

Corbett smiled when she looked up at him. Never would he become so jaded that he would not be entranced by the color of her eyes. Even during the four years he had spent in

London, surrounded by lovely, willing ladies, he could summon the color of her eyes to mind at will. In fact, he had done so frequently, always reminding himself that no one had eyes the color of Penelope's. The pale blue gown that she had worn yesterevening had only accentuated their green hue. Tonight, in the light of one flickering candle, her pale yellow gown made her eyes shine with a glow all their own.

He was glad, too, that she had undone that wretched plait. Her silken gold tresses, disheveled from her weeping, fell softly about her shoulders and down her back. Was this what she would look like some morning, upon arising from his bed after a night spent in lovemaking? He drew in a deep breath to calm the bounding leap that his heart—not to mention other parts of his anatomy—had made upon this speculation.

Of course, before he could enjoy these prospects, there was one great obstacle to be surmounted, an obstacle that had lain between them for four long years. Now was his opportunity, with a simple explanation, to destroy forever the barriers that separated them.

Corbett took a deep breath and began, "Bradley and I have been seeking you everywhere, Penelope. I am glad I found you first."

"Please do not take offense, Corbett," she said with a wry little smile, "but I am sorry anyone found me at all."

"We were greatly concerned for you, Penelope," Corbett said.

"I am sure Mrs. Dilley was the most concerned of all," she said sarcastically.

"That wretched old cat purposefully intended to embarrass you tonight," he said angrily.

"She succeeded admirably."

"'Twas reprehensible of her."

"No, she is correct, Corbett," Penelope said. "I do not know which spoon to use or even how to play a simple little song on the piano, much less some of the complicated things Margaret and the other ladies played. I saw all those notes.

Why, the paper was fairly black with them—and I have no idea what a one of them meant! Who am I trying to fool with my grand airs?" she demanded, plucking at the lace along the bodice of her borrowed gown. "Passing myself off as a fine lady when I am really just a stupid, ignorant country girl."

"You most assuredly are not stupid nor ignorant!" he protested.

"Reading every book in the Reverend Mr. Wroxley's study might have been very interesting, but it did not prepare me to be an earl's daughter."

"Indeed," Corbett replied with a chuckle. "I would wager very few daughters of noblemen have read more than three books in their entire lives—and at that, I believe myself to be estimating most generously."

She pressed her lips tightly together and leaned her head wistfully to the side. "'Tis not solely Mrs. Dilley. Everyone knows I do not belong here, Corbett."

"Lord Bellingsford says you belong here," he reminded her. "That should be enough to satisfy anyone."

"It does not satisfy Mrs. Dilley," she protested.

Corbett made a little noise of disgust. Recalling how Mrs. Dilley tried to badger even the indomitable Margaret, he could just imagine how forceful the lady would appear to someone as sheltered and shy as Penelope.

"Would anything truly please Mrs. Dilley?" he asked. "At any rate, that lady has reasons of her own to be displeased, reasons that should not concern you."

"Corbett," she said, looking into his eyes intently, "I know you mean well, but you of all people should be able to see that I do not belong here. You know very well were it not for your help I would not have been able to eat dinner yester-evening without making a fool of myself. For all they were expecting of me, I may as well have just picked up the bowl and drunk the soup!" she declared.

Corbett chuckled. "Then I would have done so, too—just

so you would not be the first to steal a march on a new fashion."

At last, Penelope smiled. Corbett could not resist the impulse to reach out and smooth his index finger across the dark semicircles beneath her eyes. He let his fingers linger on her pale cheek. He raised his hand to gently lift a stray strand of flaxen hair from her forehead. His fingers brushed slowly through her soft hair until his hand rested upon her shoulder. The gesture might be interpreted as merely comforting—although he hoped she would realize he meant it to be so much more.

"I would wager you have not slept very well the past two nights," he said. "That is why you are so overset. Things won't seem so bleak once you are rested. And you *will* sleep better, once you have become accustomed to being here."

Corbett moved his hand slowly over her shoulder to her arm. He smoothed his hand up and down her arm, easing the delicate lace which fell from her shoulder farther out of the way each time until he could feel her warm, bare skin beneath his touch. Her cheeks were soft, her smooth arms even softer. How he longed to allow his hands to continue their journey over the entire length of her body, just to ascertain if other parts of her were equally as soft and smooth.

"Penelope." Corbett at last summoned the courage he needed to broach this most important subject. "You know I am always willing to help you. By now, do you not know why?"

CHAPTER
NINE

"I HAVE BEGUN to think, of late, that you measured everything by pounds and pence," she admitted. "I cannot think of what use I am to you."

"I have been wanting to speak to you privately ever since you arrived—no, even before you arrived at Bellford Manor," Corbett said. "I have wanted to tell you—to try to explain to you—for four years I have wanted to explain. . . ."

Corbett cursed himself for stuttering and stammering over the words that he had practiced to himself countless times. Why must he turn into a burbling idiot now?

"You need not explain a thing, Corbett," she said. "I know what happened."

Corbett shook his head. "I should still like you to hear my version."

He was glad when Penelope turned to face him. At this moment, he did not want to waste time explaining anything. He just wanted to wrap her soft body in his arms and cover her face with kisses until he could make her his own, just as he had always wanted to do. With a heavy sigh, he restrained his impulse.

"Four years ago," he began, "my father inherited a title—"

"I *know* that, Corbett," she interrupted.

"And I received instructions to marry an heiress." He waited for some response from her. When there was none, he continued, "There are plenty of heiresses to be had in exchange for a title, Penelope. Did you ever wonder why, in four years, I still have not married?"

Penelope shook her head yes, then no, then merely shrugged.

"Long ago I found the lady I wished to marry, yet her lack of fortune and my duty to my family kept us apart. Do you take my meaning, Penelope?" he asked. His grasp tightened about her arm, as if he were afraid she would flee from him.

"I understand," she murmured. "I understand more than you think I do."

"When I discovered that you were Lord Bellingsford's daughter, and an heiress, all the barriers which kept us apart were broken. At last, I can marry the lady I have loved all along. Do you truly understand what I am trying to say to you?"

"I understand that, were it not for my inheritance, you would never have sought me out again. How convenient for you." Abruptly, she wrenched her arm from his grasp and rose from the sofa. "Forgive me for not accommodating you in your ambitions."

Stunned, Corbett opened his mouth to protest, but she began to move away from him. "I should not be here alone with you, Corbett."

Well, he had not exactly expected her to fall swooning into his arms. She was not the type of lady who swooned, and he was not precisely the type of gentleman ladies swooned over—even if, in all modesty, he did consider himself devilishly handsome. On the other hand, considering the way she had seemed to adore him from afar when they were younger, he had rather expected her at least to be happy once he had explained everything to her fully—perhaps even to have allowed him to embrace her or kiss her. He had never expected she would want to run away from him.

Corbett was so shocked by this completely unexpected response that Penelope was halfway across the room before he could even rise from the sofa.

"You must not leave now, Penelope," he said, rising to

follow her. "Not like this. There are still so many things I need to explain to you."

"That does not signify," she answered, still backing away from him. "'Tis not proper for a lady to be alone with a gentleman other than her father or brother."

"Or betrothed?" Corbett offered.

Penelope paused and swallowed hard before replying. "As you are none of the above-mentioned, I must bid you good evening."

"I could be, Penelope," he said as he moved to follow her.

She turned to face him. Her eyes were slivers of pale green ice. "No, you cannot. Never."

Quickly, Penelope left the sitting room. She was not sure where she was going, but any place was preferable to here.

Merciful heavens! she cried to herself as she made her way down the endless corridors. Corbett had made her an offer of marriage! She could hardly believe it to be true. What was more incredible, she could hardly believe she had rebuffed him.

The very possibility that such a thing might happen brought her headache back with a vengeance. How she had once longed to have him love her! Fool that she was for him, she might even have considered the possibility of being his without benefit of clergy, if he had ever asked.

'You should turn about immediately,' some little part inside of her tempted. 'Return to him and accept his offer, whatever it is. What does it matter that he is only marrying you for your newly-acquired fortune? At last, you will have the man you have always loved.'

'Not like that,' Penelope vowed to herself, and thrust aside all her temptations. She drew in a deep breath of renewed determination, and continued on toward her bedchamber. 'Twas true, she had no social graces or accomplishments. What education she possessed had come solely from the Reverend Mr. Wroxley's generosity toward her regarding her use of his limited library. But regardless of her station in life, she possessed her pride—and pride would not allow her to be married off for her fortune.

"The devil take Corbett Remington for even thinking that I could be!" she muttered to herself as she entered her bed-chamber.

She pressed her lips resolutely together. She closed her eyes, then allowed herself one brief moment of regret as she lifted her chin proudly and closed the door tightly behind her.

In her bedchamber the next morning, Penelope stood abso-lutely still atop a green velvet footstool. The formidable Mme. Dupres directed the stoop-shouldered, squint-eyed seamstress who knelt at Penelope's feet, pinning lengths of lace to the hem of a white silk gown. Like some lunatic but-terfly let loose in a field of fantastic flowers, Margaret flitted from one brilliant bolt of cloth to another. Margaret's abigail, and a strangely quiet Gwenyth, stood in a far corner, observ-ing everything.

All Penelope dared move was her eyes. If she looked to the left, she could see her bed. When she looked straight ahead, she could marvel at her own well-dressed reflection in the large, gilt-framed pier glass. If she turned her glance to the right, she could see how Margaret watched her with ad-miration, all the while keeping the modiste under censorious surveillance.

"Oh, just look at you!" Margaret exclaimed. "You are so pretty."

Indeed, she hardly recognized herself, Penelope thought. Yet deep inside, she still worried about what everyone else there would think of the change in her.

"Margaret, beneath all these fine things, I am still just plain Penelope Graves."

Margaret shook her head with great conviction, then gig-gled. "Oh, no. You are Lady Ermentrude Fairmount. You will never be just plain Penelope Graves again."

Penelope silently debated whether this was something to be celebrated or mourned.

"I think what has happened to you is simply wonderful!" Margaret continued enthusiastically. "Regardless of the extent of one's fortune, you are something I shall never be—a lady born."

"No lady born to the title could ever be more kind to me than you have been," Penelope told her. She was surprised to see Margaret actually blush—profusely—at this compliment.

"So, Lord Bellingsford drew me aside after breakfast," Margaret declared rather loudly, as if to drive Penelope's unwarranted praise from the room. " 'Someone very special is coming for Ermentrude today,' he told me. I said, 'She'll consider them special only if they do not call her Ermentrude.' "

Penelope giggled.

"At any rate," Margaret continued her tale, "his lordship thanked me for lending you my gowns, but he insisted you must have some of your own. Therefore, he asked me—just *me*, mind you, none of the other ladies—to help you when he summoned Mme. Dupres from the village to provide you with what you will need until you get to London."

"I believe Mme. Dupres has misunderstood Lord Bellingsford's instructions," Penelope remarked, glancing about at the bedazzling display in her bedchamber. "I would wager there is enough fabric here to clothe half of London."

Having only worn simple gowns she and her mother had made of the cheapest of materials, Penelope was quite overwhelmed with what Mme. Dupres offered. In addition to bolts of muslin, silk, velvet, wool, and brocade, there were yards of braid, ribbon, and a dozen varieties of imported lace. There were fine chemises, and sheer pink hose, and tiny slippers cut so low that, until Margaret showed her how to tie the satin ribbons about her instep and ankles, Penelope feared they would fall off with her first step.

In spite of the attraction of all the new finery, after several hours Penelope grew weary of standing. She stretched her arms and shoulders and tried to flex her aching knees. "When can I sit down?" she asked. She raised her arm in an attempt to stifle a yawn.

"Non! Non!" Mme. Dupres warned. "Do not move or, *Hélas!* I shall prick you again with the pin."

Margaret leaned closer to Penelope, and in what Penelope was certain the girl meant to be a whisper, murmured, "If that accent is genuine, I shall eat a monkey—raw—with all his fur!"

"Are you *that* certain?" Penelope asked with a surprised giggle.

"My abigail told me that the milkmaid told her that Mme. Dupres came here from Manchester, and is no more French than Dan Wilkins' hogs," Margaret explained. "She was someone's mistress until he tired of her and set her up as a modiste. She acquired the accent to give her business a little cachet. Still, I cannot say I blame her, do you?"

Penelope merely shrugged, and was rewarded with a pinprick.

"Hélas! I did warn you," Mme. Dupres said with a deep sigh.

"Mme. Dupres, can we not stop? I am awfully tired," Penelope said. "We have already measured three gowns—"

"Non, non. It is not finished," Mme. Dupres protested. "You require too many things to rest now. Three more gowns, *tout au moins!*"

"Three more?" Penelope could not begin to imagine where she could possibly wear the three gowns she had already ordered, much less three additional gowns.

"Mais oui! And a pelisse—no, two," Mme. Dupres continued her avaricious inventory. "A riding habit, you must have it."

"But I do not ride!" Penelope protested. "And two evening gowns should be enough. While one is being cleaned, I can wear the other."

"Madame, you are not *folle furieuse!*" Mme. Dupres

scolded, encircling her temple with her index finger. "You must know you cannot be seen in the same two gowns again and again."

"But—" Completely befuddled by now, Penelope looked to Margaret for support.

Margaret firmly shook her head and leaned toward Penelope as if to whisper in her ear. Margaret was incapable of whispering. "Buy only what you need. Wait until you get to London to see the latest styles—and a bit better workmanship," she added after fingering the sleeve of Penelope's gown.

"*Non, non, Madame* cannot go to London looking like this," Mme. Dupres protested. "She needs not just a few gowns, but an entire new wardrobe. If all this does not suit, I have so much more."

"*C'est tout! Nous n'achetons plus. Vas-t'en avec ce que tu as déjà!*" Margaret released a flood of what was to Penelope completely unintelligible scoldings. "*Veux-tu que je dise à* Lord Bellingsford *que*—"

Mme. Dupres' brown eyes grew round with surprise. Before Margaret could finish, the modiste had scooped up the gowns she had already fitted and quickly hustled the seamstress from the room.

Penelope looked on in complete awe. "What on earth did you say to her?"

Margaret burst out laughing and collapsed into an empty chair. "I would wager that the so-called Mme. Dupres does not know what I said either."

"But what did you—"

"I merely told the greedy wretch that we would buy no more, and to go away with what she already had," Margaret explained. "I was about to ask if she wanted Lord Bellingsford to know how unsatisfactory her work was, but she left too quickly."

"How did you learn—"

Margaret shrugged. "Oh, even the frog language is useful

from time to time when one's father is in the business of . . . importing."

Penelope began to regret having thought Margaret merely a shatter-brained ninnyhammer.

Margaret walked about the bedchamber, drawing the draperies closed. "Come now. You look quite exhausted, Penelope. Why do you not have a nice nap before dinner?" she suggested as she tiptoed out of the room.

Penelope was so exhausted and her legs hurt her so badly that she did not even bother to make the short walk to retrieve her dressing gown from the bed. She collapsed into the nearest empty chair, clad only in her thin chemise.

'All my life, I have walked everywhere I went and never felt badly,' she thought as she wiggled her toes and ankles and rubbed her cramped legs. 'Why, now, after one horseback ride and one morning of standing, should I suffer so?'

Ah well, at least by enduring this torment, she thought rather philosophically, she had been released from yet another obligatory morning ride.

At last the pain began to subside. She let her head fall against the back of the chair and closed her eyes. How good it felt to sit! As exhaustion swept over her, at last she slept.

The light touch on her bare shoulder woke her.

"Bradley!" She scrambled to sit up, slapping at his hand so that he had to draw it back quickly. She had not heard him enter. "How dare you walk in on me without knocking!"

She wrapped her arms about herself and quickly jumped from the chair. She ran to her bed for the covering protection of her dressing gown.

Bradley made a great show of gallantly turning his back to her, but Penelope could not help but notice that he had strategically placed himself in a position to view her half-dressed figure in the long pier glass. She warily watched Bradley as she tied the narrow belt securely about her waist.

Seeing that she was now decently covered, Bradley turned to face her. His fair head lowered, he looked up at her with extraordinarily apologetic eyes.

"But I *did* knock, several times, too," he earnestly protested his innocence. "You were obviously too deeply asleep to hear me."

Penelope pressed her lips together and considered the veracity of his statement. 'Twas true, she had been exhausted enough not to have heard his knock.

"I was quite concerned for you, you know," Bradley said. His brow was creased with worry. "When I received no response to my knock, I feared you had fallen ill. You truly have not looked too well lately, even before your fall from Merriwether. Are you certain you did not have some bad prawns that first evening?"

Penelope shook her head.

"Forgive me, little cousin, if, in my impetuousness to be certain you were well, I have offended you. When I entered your room, I had no idea you would be in a state of deshabille."

"That does not signify. Once having seen me like this, you should have left immediately."

Bradley gave her a mischievous grin. "My dear little cousin, I am only human—and you are very lovely."

Penelope sighed with exasperation. "What do you want, Bradley?"

"'Tis time for luncheon," he announced brightly. With a little chuckle, he continued, "I know what difficulties you have in finding your way about this enormous house. I stopped by your bedchamber to ask if you needed any help in finding your way to the dining room."

"That is very kind of you, Bradley. However, 'tis becoming increasingly easy to find my way about this place on my own. I shan't be needing your help."

"Then at least allow me to accompany you."

"I shan't be going down to luncheon. All these fittings have made me so tired. . . ."

"Then you will be spending the afternoon in your bedchamber?' he asked. He still smiled, but Penelope noticed the barest lift of one fair brow.

"Yes. And the door will be locked! Go away, Bradley."

"There is no reason to be so unfriendly, my dear little cousin," he complained in greatly injured tones. "I cannot help if I am a slave in my devotion to you. If only you would give me the chance to prove to you that all I want is to be near you."

Penelope was too exhausted to listen to his foolish flatteries. She shook her head. Hoping to dismiss him quickly, she carelessly quipped, "Be near me somewhere else—and some other time."

"Some other time?" Bradley seized the phrase. "Does this mean that I may still hope that you will one day return the deep affection I feel for you?"

"It means that right now, I am tired. Go away, Bradley," she wearily ordered him.

"But someday you will not be tired of me," Bradley persisted.

Slowly, he approached her from across the room. Penelope continued to retreat until her back was against the window, and she could go no farther.

Bradley stood before her, blocking any attempt at flight. "In the fervent hope for the rapid realization of that day, might I be so bold as to ask you now to do me the great honor of bestowing upon me your hand in marriage?"

"Marriage?" Penelope repeated incredulously.

"Marriage," Bradley repeated emphatically. "I wish you to be my wife. I will be an excellent husband to you. I am extremely generous. Just ask any lady."

Penelope blinked, bewildered. She had fallen asleep in the chair and all this was merely an extraordinarily strange dream, bordering on the nightmarish, actually. Yes, that could be the only logical explanation for what she was hearing—or what she was dreaming she was hearing—just now.

"I am certain Uncle Roger will consent," Bradley said as further inducement.

Penelope swallowed hard. "I thank you for the offer, Bradley," she replied. "But, I cannot marry you."

"Of course you can marry me. Uncle Roger—"

"It has nothing to do with Uncle . . . Lord . . . my father," she said. "I cannot marry a man I do not love."

Bradley stepped forward and seized her hand. The touch of his fingers upon her made her realize that this was not a dream.

"Oh, Lord help me!" she cried, as much in exasperation as in disgust. "You are not about to try to attack me again, are you?"

"Penelope, can you not forget my shameful drunken behavior?" he cried. "You see I am quite sober now and quite in earnest in my proposal."

"You only want to marry me for my fortune!" Penelope accused, rapidly withdrawing her hand.

Bradley stared at her incredulously. "Penelope, some sad day, upon Uncle Roger's inevitable demise, I shall be an earl." He gestured about her room, but Penelope knew he truly meant to encompass all of Bellford Manor and its environs. "All this will be mine. I do not need your fortune." He turned to face her, again seizing her hands in his. "Marry me, Penelope."

"No, Bradley. I will not marry you," she insisted.

"You are surprised by my offer, and too exhausted to think clearly," Bradley said, nodding his head. Slowly, he began to move away from her, across the bedchamber. "I should not have spoken so precipitously. I shall give you more time to consider my most honorable proposal."

"I do not need any more time, Bradley," she said. "My answer will be the same."

"We shall see," Bradley replied as he headed for the door.

As he closed the door behind him, a wave of relief swept over Penelope. As exhausted as she was, she still ran to the door, made certain it was closed tightly, then locked it securely—just to be safe. With a sigh of relief, she returned to the bed and collapsed into a fitful sleep.

* * *

"I take it you'll be wanting the brandy, sir," Jakes said to him as Bradley entered his bedchamber.

Bradley nodded and slumped into a chair by the fireside. "Is my disappointment at my cousin's refusal so evident on my face, Jakes?"

"My first clue was when you kicked the cat upon entering, sir," Jakes answered, handing him a snifter of brandy. He set the crystal decanter down upon the table beside Bradley.

"She refused me, Jakes!" Bradley exclaimed in disbelief. "How could she refuse me?"

Jakes shook his head. "'Tis beyond me, sir. Had you been drinking before you asked her?"

"Of course not!" Bradley said as he downed another gulp of the brandy.

"Did you have onions with your luncheon?"

"I have not eaten luncheon yet."

Jakes shook his head as he watched Bradley down yet another snifterful. "Don't look as if you'll be taking luncheon today, neither—not off a plate, at any rate,"

"Well, I shall simply have to try again tomorrow," Bradley said. As he watched the amber liquid swirling in the glass, his hope renewed. "Or the next day. She'll come 'round."

"I hope so, sir," Jakes said. "Just today at the *Crown and Boar*, I spotted them two bookmakers from Cheapside—"

"You cannot mean—what is his name, Tate, and that ugly fellow Borden?"

"Indeed, I do, sir. Them what you're into for—"

Bradley quickly raised his hand to stop Jakes. "No, no. Do not remind me. Do you suppose the story has got 'round already? Now I shall have all the duns at my door."

"From what I've heard, sir, these two don't like to use the duns. They prefer to rely upon their own considerably persuasive talents."

"Oh, Jakes, why is everyone here acting as if they are so glad to see Penelope?" Bradley demanded. "Why are they all acting as if her sudden reappearance has not changed their lives one iota when she has completely ruined mine?"

"Well, perhaps not completely, sir," Jakes reassured him. "Perhaps just inconvenienced temporarily."

"If Tate and Borden catch me, I could be inconvenienced permanently!" Bradley frowned. "What am I going to do if she will not marry me?"

Jakes pursed his lips and looked about to the corners of the room, as if trying to distract Bradley's attention from himself. Then he smiled. "You could always take her riding again, sir."

Bradley frowned up at Jakes through the hazy glow that the brandy was beginning to impart to his surroundings. "Again? She will not get on that horse again."

"Then I'll just persuade the stable boys to find me another skittish horse."

"'Twas your doing?" Bradley said. A wide grin began to spread across his face as he realized what his valet was about.

Jakes gave him a smug grin. "Where would I be without you, sir? A man has to watch which side his bread's buttered on, if you take my meaning."

Bradley took another drink and shook his head. "Here, all this time, I had thought Mrs. Dilley had stuck the horse with a hat pin." He raised his glass to Jakes. "I am beginning to think giving you this position was not a complete waste of time after all, Jakes."

CHAPTER
TEN

"I AM QUITE prepared to enjoy myself this morning," Margaret announced to Lord Ormsley as she drew her horse to a stop beside his.

"But, Miss Dilley, I thought you did not enjoy riding," his lordship said.

"Well, I do not. But I intend to spend the morning sitting here, telling you all the wonderful gossip my abigail has told me, and *that* I do enjoy."

"As do I," Lord Ormsley responded with a hearty laugh. "Tell me, Miss Dilley, I saw Lord Forbush leaving here and he was not backing away from everyone, therefore I assume that he must have had his breeches mended. Pray, how did he manage to do it?"

"Would you believe Miss Stamish persuaded her abigail to sew them?"

"How delighted Lady Forbush must be," Lord Ormsley remarked.

Margaret leaned just a bit closer to his lordship and whispered, "I do not think she knows yet how they got to be mended—and *I* shan't be the one to tell her."

Lord Ormsley nodded his head in Lady Forbush's direction. Her matronly figure resplendent in a bright red velvet riding habit, she was seated atop her black gelding, chatting merrily with several handsome young gentlemen. "I, for one, do not think she gives a fig how it happened—so long as his lordship is gone."

"She does look happy to be . . . riding," Margaret agreed. She threw Lord Ormsley a knowing little wink.

Mrs. Dilley drew her horse up beside Margaret's. With her riding crop, she dealt her daughter a short jab in the ribs, just to emphasize the point she wished to make. "So does Corbett, my dear," she said. "He is an exceptionally good horseman, is he not, my lord?"

"Oh, indeed," Lord Ormsley answered. "Been riding ever since he was a little shaver."

"Why do you not go ride with him, Margaret?" Mrs. Dilley suggested.

"But, he appears to be so busy at the moment that I hate to bother him," Margaret answered. "And I do believe the poor man has his work cut out for him." She shook her head sadly, yet nevertheless gave a quiet little giggle. "Oh, poor Mr. Remington. Poor Ermentrude, too."

Mrs. Dilley laughed loudly as she watched Penelope trying to transfer herself from the mounting block to a different horse, this time a small bay mare. Corbett and the groom were trying to assist her, without much success.

Penelope turned from her concentration upon placing her foot in the stirrup and watched Mrs. Dilley with growing concern. To what additional ridicule would that horrid woman subject her today?

"Pay them no mind, Lady Ermentrude," Corbett told her softly. "You *can* do it."

Penelope shot him a glare of disbelief. She was not certain she remembered how she had managed to mount the last time, even in the privacy of the stables. She greatly doubted that she could repeat the process successfully, much less do so gracefully—especially knowing that everyone was watching her, just waiting for her to make a mistake.

She was doing this for one—and only one—reason. To prove to Mrs. Dilley, and anyone else who might doubt that she had any business being the daughter of an earl, that she truly *did* belong here at Bellford Manor—and not merely as a servant.

Lord Bellingsford, or even Bradley, or any number of the young gentlemen house guests, would have been more than eager to assist her.

But why was she allowing Corbett to help her? she asked of herself. Penelope had to think a bit longer to find the answer to that question. She dared not dig too deeply inside, for fear of what response she should find. There was only one reason that she could safely admit to herself.

She needed to be able to conduct herself like a genuine lady as much as Corbett needed to marry an heiress. If Corbett thought he could use her to obtain her fortune, then she might as well use him to teach her how she ought to behave. That seemed a fair enough exchange.

At any rate, it prevented her from thinking about her real reasons for accepting his assistance. She did not want to acknowledge how much she still cared for Corbett, in spite of how badly he had hurt her. This way, she need not admit that she would use almost any excuse to still be near him, no matter how much she hated him now.

Apparently Corbett thought her safely stationed upon her horse. He left her to mount his own, then leaned over to her to demonstrate the proper grip.

"You must hold the reins like this, Lady Ermentrude," he told to her.

His strong fingers, warm against hers even through the fine leather gloves, gently intertwined the reins with her fingers. Oh, why did this man's very touch make her forget what a perfidious wretch he was? she lamented. She tried all the harder to concentrate on how to manage her horse.

"This way, you will retain complete control over little Persephone here," Corbett explained.

Penelope gave him a skeptical glance and shifted her weight, the better to keep her balance in the uncomfortable sidesaddle. "I do not feel as if I have complete control over my own actions, much less those of this horse."

"You will learn," he assured her.

"And anyway, Persephone was the one that was carried off to Hades, was she not?" she reminded him.

Corbett grinned and shook his head. " 'Twas not upon a horse. You are quite safe."

"See here, lad, slow down!" one of the grooms shouted to the village boy who was running toward them. "You'll scare the horses."

"Oh, sir, there's such a commotion at the sexton's cottage!" the boy exclaimed. "I'm sent to find Miss Graves what's become a lady now."

Penelope turned so quickly that she almost toppled off Persephone. "Mama and Papa! Are they all right?" she demanded of the breathless boy.

He turned to her and gave her an appraising look. "Oh, you must be the one. Yes, m'lady. They sent me for you."

"I must go to them immediately!" Penelope said.

"Wait, Ermentrude," Lord Bellingsford said. "I shall have another groom accompany you."

She tried desperately to turn Persephone in the direction of the sexton's cottage. The harder she pulled upon first one rein and then the other, the more confused the horse became regarding precisely what Penelope expected of her. The little bay mare turned first this way, then that, placing Penelope in danger of falling out of the saddle.

"You are meeting with little success, my dear cousin. Allow me to escort you to the sexton's cottage," Bradley said as he came up in front of her.

Persephone shied as Bradley reached for her bridle. Penelope, still terrified of another bolting horse and wild ride, dropped the reins and clung to the horse's mane.

Suddenly Corbett seized Penelope firmly about her waist. With very little effort, he lifted her out of her own saddle and swung her about behind him.

"Can you ride behind me?" Corbett asked.

Penelope was scared to death up so high on Corbett's horse. The beast was so much taller than anything to which either of her two little mares ever could have aspired! She grasped the back of Corbett's jacket, leaned over, and ventured a peek down at the ground far below.

"My gracious, he is so tall," she said.

Corbett chuckled softly. "Are you afraid?"

"If my little cousin is afraid, I shall arrange to have a carriage convey her to the cottage," Bradley offered.

Penelope lifted her chin. "I most certainly am not afraid! And we must hurry. I have no time to wait for a carriage."

"We shall travel faster my way," Corbett assured her. Nevertheless, Penelope had the distinct impression he was actually informing Bradley.

"I would ride with Lucifer himself if he would get me to their cottage quickly enough," Penelope told Corbett. "Let us be off!"

"I will get you there quickly enough," he told her. "And, in all humility, I do think I am far better company than Lucifer or Bradley."

Penelope cast him a wry glance. "We are wasting time discussing your humility. Let us go."

"Place your arms about me and hold on," he warned her as he urged his horse out of the stableyard at a trot.

She was reluctant to touch him. Could she not simply hold on to the fabric of his jacket? Must she wrap her arms about his slim waist? Must she feel his firm stomach moving against her hands while her breasts pressed more closely into his muscular back with each stride of the horse? She thought of all the times she had only been able to dream of holding him when she believed she could not have him. How could she hold him now—now, when she *would* not have him?

As they left the yard, Corbett urged his horse into a gallop. Penelope clasped her arms about Corbett's tapering waist just in time to avoid being thrown off backward. She felt his back and shoulders quivering against her breasts in a silent chuckle.

"Oh, do stop laughing at me," she threatened, "or I do not know how much longer I can resist poking you in the ribs."

Corbett chuckled again—quite deliberately too. "But you

will not," he answered her confidently. "In order to poke me, you would have to release your grasp, and if you do that you will surely fall off."

Penelope frowned with consternation. She did not want to test his theory for fear he should prove correct. Well, she reasoned, if she could not release her grasp to give him his much-deserved poke, she would do the next best thing. Penelope held onto Corbett all the more tightly.

"You do realize, of course," Corbett told her in short gasps, "that if I lose consciousness from lack of oxygen, both you and I will tumble from this horse?"

"Yes," she replied defiantly. In spite of her firm belief that Corbett deserved to suffer, she *did* want to arrive at her parents' cottage without injuring herself. She eased her hold— but not too much.

After all, not only were they riding too high, they were traveling much faster than human beings should be allowed to go, Penelope decided as she watched the world fly past her in a blur.

Corbett reined his horse to a halt before the small cottage. Penelope felt a great wave of relief wash over her when she saw both the aging Mr. Graves and the bewildered Mrs. Graves standing, safe and well, beside Constable Swift.

Without waiting for Corbett's assistance to dismount, Penelope impulsively jumped down. She landed on her feet, but her momentum caused her to continue forward, throwing her to her knees. Quickly she sprang up. She wiped the dirt from her hands, but did not even bother to brush the grass and leaves from her new riding habit before she dashed to where Mr. and Mrs. Graves and Constable Swift were standing. They stared down at the pile of charred rubble that had once been the chicken coop.

"Constable, you've got to find who did this. They must be punished!" Mr. Graves insisted.

Constable Swift brushed an invisible fleck of lint from his lapel. "How can we punish them when we don't even know who they are?"

"Of course we know who they are!" Penelope interrupted as she made her way to stand by the elderly sexton's side. " 'Twas the same ones that put goose grease all over the ropes Papa uses for lowering the coffins and created such a fuss last spring when old Squire Wilkins was buried."

Penelope heard Corbett coughing as if trying to hide his chuckle as he came up behind her. She shot her elbow out backward to catch him in the ribs.

"Well, now, that *was* quite a to-do," Constable Swift acknowledged with a laugh. "But that was just a boyish prank. Come now, Graves, you've seen enough of them over the years to know—"

"No! Putting toads in the milk pitcher and red madder in the laundry were just boyish pranks," Mr. Graves insisted. "Eating my porridge dry and wearing pink unmentionables for over a month was merely annoying."

Constable Swift chuckled—the callous wretch! Penelope wanted to slap the smirk from his pudgy face. 'Twas not *his* breakfast nor *his* clothing that had been ruined.

Mr. Graves jabbed his grimy, stubby finger at the ashen remains of the coop. "But this is more than a silly trick. *This* was downright dangerous!"

"Mr. Graves is correct, Constable," Corbett said. "The other pranks all seemed to be merely the work of naughty little boys, just showing a bit of mischief. Considering how long this has been going on, some of them are grown now, and probably hard-working men in the village—why, very like yourself, Constable, no doubt."

"But the ones what did this . . . no, they're mean beyond redemption, they are," Mr. Graves declared. "You've *got* to find these boys and stop them. They've got to be punished!"

"You don't believe they truly meant any harm this time any more than they ever did?" the constable asked. " 'Twas probably a prank that just got out of hand, accidental-like. I doubt you'll have to worry about it happening again."

"Of course not," Mr. Graves grumbled, staring at the blackened remains. "We've nothing else for them to burn down—unless they want to try next for the whole blasted house."

"Constable Swift, you cannot leave it at this," Penelope insisted, glaring at him. "You *must* do something."

"What can I do, Miss Penelope—or Lady Ermentrude—or whoever they think you are this week?" Constable Swift asked with a subtle sneer.

"I am Lady Ermentrude Fairmount," she informed him haughtily. For the first time since her strange new life had begun, she actually *felt* the authority she conveyed. "And as constable, 'tis your duty to see that the culprits are apprehended. If you cannot perform your duty properly, I am certain a competent officer can readily be found to replace you."

Constable Swift stepped back a pace and stared at her in amazement. He removed his cap and replied sheepishly, "For as long as I can remember—long before you were born, m'lady—the village boys have been playing these silly tricks. Ain't no way to tell which boys they were, and no way to prove it, neither. All these years and we ain't never been able to find any of them. Like as not, we never will."

Penelope could have screamed with frustration.

Constable Swift tipped his hat to the group and walked away.

"Oh, Mama, Papa! This is so terrible!" Penelope exclaimed, falling into Mrs. Graves' motherly arms.

"Well, it could've been worse," Mr. Graves acknowledged, still shaking his head. "At least the stupid chickens had the sense to get out of the burning coop."

"Such a pity, such a pity," Mrs. Graves mumbled. She stared at the charred debris and sadly shook her head. "Such a pity they all got out. I truly would favor a nice roast chicken dinner right about now."

"What have you done with the surviving chickens, Mr. Graves?" Corbett asked.

The wizened old man grimaced, then jerked his gray head in the direction of his cottage. "We've tried to keep them in the lean-to what used to be Penelope's bedroom, sir, but they've wandered their way into the kitchen. Oh, b'gads, what a mess! What with feathers and droppings."

"How soon will you be able to rebuild?"

Mr. Graves shook his head. "Don't know, sir. Take some time."

"The people of the village are generous," Corbett said. "When they know of your loss, I am sure they will want to help you to rebuild your coop."

Mr. Graves snorted angrily. "The ones what did this last night is some of the same ones that'll give us their castoffs tomorrow and think themselves so righteous in the giving!"

"Then perhaps Lord Bellingsford . . .?" Corbett suggested.

"His lordship got what he wanted from us," Mr. Graves said bitterly.

"I shall come home, Papa," Penelope cried impulsively. "I shall come home and help you. Oh, I never should have left in the first place."

"Don't be a fool, girl! You belong at Bellford Manor now," he said. "Oh, why did we ever send for you? You have everything now that you should have had all your life. I won't take it away from you again."

"Papa, at least let me help you clear away—"

"In that fancy gown? Have you lost your good sense?" Mrs. Graves scolded. She shook her head and made small clucking noises as she began to pick at the braid on the sleeve. "Just look—you've got it mussed up already! Go away before you do any more damage."

"Yes, please take her back to Bellford Manor, sir," Mr. Graves said to Corbett. "Take her back where she belongs."

Penelope turned and slowly began walking toward Corbett's horse. Lord Bellingsford, and no one else, wanted her at Bellford Manor. Her own parents no longer wanted her in their home. Corbett only wanted her for her fortune. Was there nowhere else to go? she sadly wondered.

He must have thought she could not hear him, Penelope

decided. Standing beside the tall horse, she watched Corbett from out of the corner of her eye as he pulled two coins from his waistcoat pocket and handed them to Mr. Graves.

"Please take this," he said.

Mr. Graves tried to push the coins back into his hand. "I told you, sir. I'll take no more charity."

"Consider it a loan."

"A loan? We can't repay you," Mr. Graves said sadly.

"I am not expecting to be repaid," Corbett told him. "Not yet, and not in coin."

Oh, what in the world was that man talking about? Penelope wondered.

Corbett swiftly remounted, then easily pulled Penelope up to sit behind him. She was surprised to find herself much less reluctant to wrap her arms about Corbett this time as they returned to Bellford Manor. Much to her continuing surprise, there was a certain comfort in the way the warm strength of his broad back and strong shoulders came between her and the harsh realities of the world.

They rode along in silence. There was no playful banter between them this time. She realized that her concern for her parents was what had made her snappish with him during the ride to the cottage. Now, she was much too hurt and confused to engage in idle chatter. And the thing she truly wanted to talk about? Somehow, she could not bring herself to give voice to her feelings. Not yet. Not with Corbett Remington.

So many changes had taken place in her life in the past week. She had been showered with gowns and jewels and gifts of all sorts by Lord Bellingsford. She had encountered a great friend in the impetuous Margaret Dilley. She had been introduced into a wonderful new world. She had also been terrorized by Bradley and humiliated by Mrs. Dilley. She did not even want to consider how many times she had not needed anyone's help to make a fool of herself.

She pressed her face against the soft, blue velvet of Corbett's jacket. She felt his firm muscles shifting beneath the fabric in easy coordination with the horse's gait. She felt his chest slowly rising and falling with each breath. Gradually her own breathing fell into cadence with his.

The comforting rhythm of the ride finally caused her to release the turbulent emotions she had held inside for so long. Hot tears trickled, unchecked, down her cheeks, and soaked into the velvet of Corbett's jacket.

Corbett could feel her slender body quivering as she wept. He slowed his horse's pace to a walk, allowing Penelope the time to release her tears and then to compose herself before reentering Bellford Manor and confronting all the censorious eyes that awaited her there.

At last, they drew to a halt before the wide steps that lead up to the front door. Corbett dismounted, then turned to assist Penelope from the horse.

Her red-rimmed eyelids made her eyes appear more intensely green. Her nose had turned a delicate pink. She looked soft and sad and vulnerable.

"No more tears now, my lady. Both your parents are still alive—and the chickens were saved," he reminded her. He grinned, hoping to distract her from her distressing thoughts, hoping to cheer her just a little.

"I know. I am grateful my parents are safe." She sniffed once again. "And I am glad for the chickens, too."

He reached his arms up to assist her to dismount. "Then what is troubling you, Penelope?"

"Why must those people be so cruel?" she asked with a little sob as she wiped her tears away. "What did my parents ever do to them but grow old and tired cleaning their church and burying their dead?"

Corbett shook his head. How he wish he knew what fiendish essence possessed certain people to torment those less fortunate and less powerful than they.

"I have missed them so," Penelope said. "I should have gone to visit them every day, but . . . I have . . . I have been so busy. . . ." She sighed and slowly shook her head. "In truth, I have been so selfish, so enwrapped in my own amusement. . . ."

Corbett patted her hand sympathetically and nodded his agreement. " 'Tis understandable. Still, I suppose 'twould have done no harm for you to see them more often."

" 'Tis so easy for you to pass judgement, isn't it?" she demanded angrily, pulling her hand away. "All your life you've had only the best. How would you like to have nothing of your own—only the things that someone else had already used?"

Corbett blinked with surprise. What had he said wrong? He had agreed with her. Why should she suddenly be angry with him?

"Penelope, I was only trying to make you feel—"

"What do you know about people's feelings?" she snapped at him. "You are the one who cares more for your family's fortune than for a lady's heart!"

Ignoring his outstretched arms, Penelope slid from the saddle. She landed on her feet, but once again, her momentum sent her stumbling forward. This time she collided with Corbett's chest. Her palms rested against him, her head stopping just under his chin. When she raised her face to look at him, his lips were barely inches from her own.

She pushed herself away from him, and stalked past him and up the wide flight of marble steps. The footman who held the front door open for her looked almost as surprised as Corbett when she wrenched it from his hands and quickly slammed it shut behind her.

Corbett stood for a moment at the bottom of the steps beside his horse, trying to sort out in his mind what had happened.

How in the world is a man to handle a woman? he silently wondered. Why do they get angry with you when you disagree with them—and get angry with you when you agree with them, too?

Penelope stood with her head pressed against the cool, white-painted wood of the front door until she had mastered the tears that still threatened to fall. No, she decided, she had shed more than enough tears. She was determined never to cry again for Corbett Remington.

She drew in a deep breath and prepared to turn once again to face the sometimes hostile denizens of Bellford Manor. The footman had vanished. She had hoped to be alone. Instead, she saw Bradley, purposefully striding toward her across the long hall.

CHAPTER ELEVEN

"You appear dreadfully overset, little cousin," Bradley said. "I trust the old couple are well."

Penelope nodded.

"Then, has Mr. Remington done something to upset you?" he demanded. "Oh, I knew I never should have allowed you to go off with the man."

"No!" Penelope answered quickly. Too quickly, she reflected, to convince Bradley that Corbett was not the cause of her distress. More calmly, she replied, "No. Mr. Remington has nothing to do with this matter, Bradley. Nothing whatsoever."

Penelope began to walk away, hoping to reach quickly the shelter of her bedchamber.

"I am glad to hear that, little Penelope," Bradley said as he followed her. "Else I should have to give the blackguard a sound thrashing, just to teach him a lesson."

Penelope blinked in surprise and forced herself to continue walking without breaking out into laughter. 'Twas no easy task when the ludicrous image of the foppish Bradley Fairmount engaging in any sort of fisticuffs with the broad-shouldered Corbett Remington kept flashing into her mind.

"No need for that, Bradley," Penelope managed to inform him. "Mr. Remington means very little to me."

"I am glad to hear that," Bradley said. "*I* want to be the man who means more to you than anything."

Penelope made no effort to stop to listen to Bradley's bothersome babblings, but continued to wend her way down the hall. She hoped the motion might drive from her mind the disturbing fact that Corbett Remington *did* still mean so much to her.

"I want to be the man who marries you, Penelope," Bradley said. He reached out his hand and laid it upon her arm in an effort to stop her.

She pulled away from him quickly. "We have been through all this before, Bradley," she told him sternly as she continued to back away from him. Nervously, she glanced about her. Oh, how she wished someone would pass them in this long, deserted corridor. What could have possessed her to seek privacy when Bradley was following her instead of seeking the company of the crowd of house guests here at Bellford Manor? "I have told you before, I will not marry you."

"Why not? I no longer do those things which you found so abhorrent," he reminded her.

Penelope nodded. "'Tis true, you have stopped drinking so much, and you *have* been kind to me, Bradley."

"If I have stopped doing those things you found distasteful, and you will not marry me, then is there something that I do *not* do that you would want me to?" he asked.

"'Tis not what you do or do not do, Bradley," Penelope tried to explain. By way of consolation, she tried to offer, "I have come to like you, Bradley. But I do not love you."

"Then marry me, and you will learn to love me!" he cried.

"Love is a feeling you either have or you do not have, Bradley," she tried to explain something which she did not understand fully herself. "Nothing can change that."

"Nothing?"

She shook her head.

"I am very sorry to hear that, Penelope. Very, very sorry." Bradley pressed his lips together tightly, turned abruptly on his heel, and strode away from her.

Penelope watched with relief as he left. Still, a small shiver crept slowly up her back. He was not a one to let anything he wanted escape him so easily. She feared she had not heard the last of Bradley Fairmount.

Quickly, Penelope retreated to the apparent shelter of her bedchamber. Remembering the previous afternoon, when Bradley had walked in on her, she locked her door. She briefly toyed with the idea of placing a large chair before the door as well.

"A ball? Oh, I simply adore balls!" Margaret proclaimed when Lord Bellingsford announced his intentions to hold one at Bellford Manor in honor of Lady Ermentrude Fairmount. When the ladies retired after dinner, she pulled Penelope aside and exclaimed, "Don't you just adore balls, Ermentrude?"

Penelope smiled politely and nodded. What did she know of balls? She had only served here from time to time whenever Lord Bellingsford entertained. Bending over the stone sink in the large kitchen, scrubbing at pots and pans and dirty dishes, she had only been able to daydream about what transpired in the ballroom. Soon she would discover what the lords and ladies were actually doing above while she had been clearing away their dinner below.

What would it be like to be attired in an elegant ball gown of diaphanous silk, fashioned just for her? she wondered. She could picture herself, allowing Gwenyth to kneel at her feet in order to tie the ribbons of her tiny slippers while she smoothed long kid gloves over her hands and up her arms. She would descend the long marble staircase and enter the splendid candlelit ballroom at Bellford Manor. She would smile politely to all the adoring gentlemen who clamored for her attention. At last she would choose one, and take the hand of that fortunate gentleman. . . .

Penelope abruptly ceased her lovely fantasy. Why must the handsome gentleman she had envisioned bear such a striking resemblance to Corbett Remington! After all these years, would she never get that man out of her mind?

"You do not *look* as if you enjoy dancing," Margaret ventured, peering into Penelope's face as if she could read the truth written there.

Penelope quickly recovered from her daydream. "Oh, Margaret, what on earth shall I wear?" she cried.

"Did Mme. Dupres not finish the white silk ball gown?" Margaret asked.

"Everything else was completed," Penelope acknowledged. "I suppose that was, too."

"That is a simply splendid choice," Margaret reassured her. "There. One problem solved already. Now, see how simple that was."

Penelope grimaced. "It may seem simple to you, Margaret. But that does not solve the problem of what I am to say to all the people who attend. I do not know them, nor they me. Oh, Margaret, you never seem to be at a loss for words. What does one say . . . ?"

"One says nothing to them," Margaret said wisely.

"But how rude."

"In order to be thought a brilliant conversationalist, one must always ask another about their favorite subject."

"That is no help!" Penelope complained. "If I do not know these people, how am I to know their favorite subject?"

"Oh, 'tis ever the same," Margaret explained. "One's favorite subject is always one's self."

Penelope giggled. "Margaret, you make everything seem so simple, and so much fun. But there is yet another problem. . . ."

"And you must tell me of it as soon as I return," Margaret said. Her attention was drawn to the opposite end of the room.

Penelope followed Margaret's gaze to where Mrs. Dilley was standing, with Mr. Dilley and Lord Ormsley, near one of the long doors that opened onto the wide terrace.

"Oh, whatever is Mama summoning me for now?" she demanded petulantly. "I vow, she is such a vexation. I shall be exceeding glad to be married and out from under her thumb."

"Then you will be subject to your husband," Penelope reminded her.

"Me? Oh, pooh! I am not a one to be under any man's thumb. I intend to find one who can be wrapped about my little finger!" Margaret declared emphatically.

Penelope unshakably believed that Margaret would.

"And, after all, Lord Ormsley is there too, and he is exceedingly pleasant company." Margaret pressed Penelope's hand between her own two. "Do not worry about the ball. Everything will work out well. You'll see."

As Penelope watched Margaret's retreating figure, she chuckled.

"You find Miss Dilley's philosophy laughable?" Corbett asked as he appeared from behind the large marble column and moved to stand beside her.

"She believes everything will work out well," Penelope repeated, then gave a bitter little sniff just to emphasize her skepticism.

"How like Miss Dilley," Corbett replied. "Upon my word, she has been blessed with the most pleasant disposition I have ever encountered."

Penelope could not help but note the affection in his voice when he spoke of Margaret. As much as Penelope agreed with Corbett, she could not help but feel a sharp twinge of jealousy to hear him express these sentiments regarding another lady.

"Have you been hiding behind columns listening to private conversations long?" Penelope asked acidly. "Or is this a recently acquired habit?"

"Quite recent, actually," Corbett replied without so much as the blink of an eye. "I am curious regarding ladies' preferences for entertainment. I believe I overheard you say you are not eagerly anticipating Lord Bellingsford's ball. Pray, why not?"

She leaned toward him—ever so slightly—and whispered, "Because then I shall have to dance."

"That usually is the purpose of a ball," Corbett reminded her with a grin.

"But I do not know how!" Penelope wailed. "Oh, there were country dances on May Day, but all I hear of now is the waltz, and I have never learned how. However on earth am I going to endure this ball without being completely mortified?"

"Is there no remedy?" Corbett asked with quite a sympathetic expression on his face.

"Of course not," Penelope said, quite resigned to her fate. "Unless I can manage to fall down and break my ankle."

Corbett frowned at her. "A rather drastic measure to avert a simple problem, don't you think?"

"Do you have a better solution?" she demanded.

"Indeed. I shall be more than happy to volunteer to teach you to dance."

Penelope stared at the floor, contemplating her alternatives. If she did not accept his offer, she would once again look a veritable fool in everyone's eyes. Nothing new there, she thought with a rueful little sniff.

And if she did accept his offer? Looking into Corbett's deep blue eyes, she knew there was no question. She would agree. She *needed* him to help her—and if he helped her, she had yet another excuse to be near him for as long as he was staying at Bellford Manor.

"Thank you, Corbett. But you must promise, no one else must ever know," she told him.

Corbett smiled. "'Twill be difficult to find a time when no one is about."

"Or a place," she added.

"I understand they are playing at forfeits tonight in the large salon. I doubt anyone will be using the ballroom."

"If I retire early, pleading another headache, I doubt I shall be missed," Penelope said with a wry twist of her delicate lips.

"Were I not leaving, too, *I* should miss you, Penelope," he told her. He reached out his hand. Before she could draw back, Corbett had taken not her hand, but merely her index and middle fingers. He ran his thumb over her smooth nails, moving across the tips at leisure.

Penelope swallowed hard. She felt as if, in that one small, simple motion, he was caressing her entire body. She swallowed again and tried to fight down the warmth rising from her breasts. Slowly, she withdrew her hand.

"I shall be waiting for you later this evening," she said. She hastily moved away.

'I shall be waiting for you later,' Penelope silently repeated her own words to herself and moaned. 'Oh, why did I say it that way? Merciful heavens! What will he think I am waiting for?'

'Shame on you! You know perfectly well what you are waiting for,' she sternly answered herself. 'And you also know perfectly well that it will never happen. Corbett is seeking you for your fortune, and will never love you as plain Penelope Graves.'

'Still, if I cannot have him, 'tis nice to pretend for a little while,' she consoled herself. Although she truly wondered if the delight in pretending was worth the hurt of returning to reality.

Penelope paced her room. She supposed that, at this time of year, 'twould be chilly in the large, empty ballroom, and she did not want to be waiting too long. How long would Corbett wait after her withdrawal before he could retire from the festivities without undue comment?

Having nothing better to do, she stood and examined her reflection in the long pier glass. Her new gown of soft, spring-green muslin dropped daringly low. Much too low, she decided, frowning. It had seemed satisfactory when she first approved the design from one of Mme. Dupres' pattern books. Of course, it was totally unsuitable now that she would be wearing it, alone, with Corbett.

She searched the wardrobe until she found a white velvet spencer. She pursed her lips. 'Twould be rather warm to wear, even for this time of year. Still, when she put it on and fastened the buttons up to her neck, she decided she could tolerate its warmth.

Margaret had arranged Penelope's hair in a mass of curls cascading from the top of her head down her back.

'Is there nothing she cannot do?' Penelope thought as she contemplated the intricate arrangement. She noted that several curls had managed to escape their confines. "Well, if Margaret can do it, so can I," she told herself with a great show of confidence.

Yet the more she tried to repin the sagging tresses, the more they came undone. At last, Penelope pulled out all the pins, and brushed her hair back into her customary knot at the base of her neck. She grimaced when she examined herself in the glass.

"I look like Penelope again," she told herself aloud. "Not Lady Ermentrude." Much to her surprise, she found she was rather sorry for it.

Still, when she stepped back and regarded the entire picture she made, she was satisfied that she looked somewhat less attractive, and she felt infinitely safer as she crept down the hall to be alone with that disturbing man.

The ballroom was chilly and just a bit damp. She was glad she had worn her concealing spencer.

"I was beginning to think you had changed your mind," Corbett said as he rose from the delicately turned chair that had been placed against the wall.

His gaze flickered up and down her figure. In his deep blue eyes, Penelope could see the gleam of the three candles set in the small candelabra that he had brought with him and placed on the table beside his chair.

"I did not change my mind," she said. She could not tell him that although she hated him for his callous fortune hunting, she would never change her mind about loving him. "Have I kept you waiting long?"

"Actually, yes," he told her with a grin. Then his eyes fixed hers with a glowing intensity. "I feel as if I have been waiting for you for an eternity, Penelope."

"Well then," she said with a bit more vigor than she ordinarily would have, "shall we start? I still remember the country dance we used to do as children. Do you?"

"Most assuredly." He held his hand out to her, inviting her to test him .

Together, they began to tread in silent time the lively steps of the dance.

Penelope giggled, as much with her nervousness as in fond remembrance. "Do you remember the time you put my bonnet on one of Squire Wilkins' piglets and danced it around? I never could remove the swinish smell from that poor bonnet."

"My apologies," he said, laughing. "Someday I shall have to replace it."

"'Tis not *proper* for a young lady to accept such a gift from a gentleman," she informed him with great dignity.

"And we do want you to appear a proper young lady, don't we?" Corbett acknowledged. "Then I shall have to wait a year—or perhaps two—until you are not quite so young."

"A year or two?" she repeated, glaring playfully at him.

"Oh, indeed." He bowed deeply to her as their dance came to an end.

The lively dance had warmed Penelope considerably. The seams of the velvet spencer began to scratch her even through the soft sarcenet lining. Corbett's presence notwithstanding, she knew she must remove it or perish with the heat. Reluctantly, she turned from Corbett and began to unfasten the small pearl buttons. As she slipped the spencer from her arms, Corbett took it from her and placed it over the back of a chair.

Unsure of how to continue, she turned to him and asked lightly, "How are my steps, Mr. Dancing Master?"

"Beautiful," he replied. She had the distinct impression,

when his eyes swept her figure, that he was referring more to her bodice than to her terpsichorean ability.

Unsettled by his gaze, Penelope returned to the dance floor. "Have you no new steps to teach me?"

"Have you ever tried this one?" Corbett asked. Once again, he began to walk her, tunelessly, through the steps of a lively quadrille.

"No," Penelope answered. Yet she found the steps simple enough to readily imitate.

"My lady, you are such an excellent dance partner, I am amazed that you were not besieged by hordes of gentlemen at the country fairs and balls."

"Corbett," she tried to explain to him, "you forget, the sexton's daughter rarely has the opportunity to attend the same affairs as young gentlemen."

Corbett pursed his lips. "Well, at any rate, at least the farmers must have . . ."

Penelope smiled her forgiveness. "They did," she admitted. "At first. But they soon gave up when they realized that I . . . I had no interest in them." She shrugged, as if that gesture should explain it all.

"Where did your interests lie, Penelope?" he asked as they completed the set of steps. "Where do they still lie?"

He did not release her hand as they both stood still, an outstretched arm's distance from each other. Slowly, he tried to draw her closer to him. Penelope resisted.

"Come now, Corbett," she said lightly, almost choking on the words she forced herself to say. "You have promised to teach me to waltz. I shan't be satisfied until you do."

"You have no idea how much I would love to see you satisfied, Penelope," Corbett told her. "But, come, I shall teach you to waltz, notwithstanding."

'Twas very difficult to continue breathing when Corbett drew her close and placed his hand upon the center of her back. 'Twas a pity she had no control over her racing heart when Corbett gazed down upon her with eyes the deep blue of the evening sky. But 'twas absolutely impossible for Penelope to remain calm when Corbett began to sway her body in synchronization with his as he moved about the room one slow step at a time. She tripped over his feet and trod upon his toes.

"Oh, I am so sorry," she cried. "'Tis so difficult to dance new steps without music."

"No need to apologize," Corbett insisted. "The fault is mine. I should have realized."

Corbett began to hum a familiar tune. Penelope found it much easier to concentrate upon the three steps when she had the rhythm of a song with which to match them. She could almost believe she was actually beginning to learn how to waltz.

Then he began to sing. Penelope started and almost fell over Corbett's feet. How could she have forgotten?

"You still sing off key," she accused.

Ignoring her complaint, Corbett continued to sing. Her laughter was mounting to the point where she was having a great deal of trouble following his lead.

"I sing like my father," Corbett defended himself quickly, then returned to his serenade.

"Oh, no. You are much worse!"

"What insupportable ingratitude!" he exclaimed. "I am kind enough to teach you to dance and you have the audacity to insult my singing?"

His eyes glowed with merriment and with another emotion Penelope readily recognized. She did not want to think he felt this way for her now—not when she had almost succeeded in closing off her heart to him.

He pulled her nearer. She could feel his firm body pressing against her, making the hot color rise from her breasts to her cheeks. He spun her about the floor until she was quite dizzy. Whether her confusion was due to the whirling motion or to Corbett's disturbing proximity, she dared not question.

She only knew that she was in his embrace, moving her

body closely against his. And she was enjoying it—immensely.

'Twas her own fault. She was paying more attention to the enjoyment of Corbett's embrace than she was to his lead. Suddenly she tripped again. Her legs became entangled not only in her own skirts, but with Corbett's legs as well. He tried to support her, but their whirling momentum was too great to stop. They both tumbled to the floor.

Corbett grunted as Penelope landed on top of him. For a moment, they both were too breathless to move. At last they each were able to draw deep breaths of revitalizing air. Penelope quickly attempted to rise. Corbett, his arms still entwined about her to cushion her fall, refused to release her.

His deep blue eyes gazed up into hers with such intense longing that Penelope ceased her efforts to rise. She lay against him, watching the way his smile lit up his ruggedly handsome face, feeling the movement of his chest as he breathed evenly, in and out.

Corbett released one of her hands. Gently, he brushed the backs of his fingers against her cheek. Continuing to stroke her ear, and the soft tendrils of hair at the side of her head, he moved his other hand to the nape of her neck, to the little knot of hair she had arranged there. He released the pins, allowing the soft golden waves to tumble down her shoulders, curtaining her face. Slowly, the gentle pressure of his hand on the back of her neck moved her face down to his.

This time, Penelope made no attempt whatsoever to resist him. His lips were warm and insistent with desire, yet tender with his love for her. She longed to stay forever in his embrace.

Slowly and carefully, he rolled her over to his side. "I have wanted to do this for so long," he whispered, caressing her face with his fingertips. Then he kissed her again.

When his lips at last parted from hers, she murmured, "I have wanted it, too, Corbett, for a long, long time."

"I need you, Penelope. Say you will marry me."

Penelope could not find the breath to answer. All she had ever wanted, from the first moment she had seen him, was now hers with a mere nod of the head. The wonderment of her dearest wish come true astonished her beyond words.

Before she could reply, he kissed her once again. He was still smiling down upon her when his eyes lit up with mischief, "I have severely compromised your honor, Lady Ermentrude. It behooves me to make an honest woman of you." He reached out to stroke her hair. "You must marry me now, do you know that?"

Penelope pulled back from him, her face frozen in stunned disbelief.

"This was a trap!" she accused.

"A trap? Why should you think . . ." Corbett demanded, bewildered. "Was it something I said?"

Her throat was so dry with horror that she could barely speak. "This was all just a devious plan to compromise my honor so I *must* marry you—and you would obtain my fortune!"

Penelope sprang to her feet, slapping her skirts into order. As he lay barely inches from her, she felt the overpowering urge to kick him!

"Penelope, I was joking!" he exclaimed.

Not listening to a single word of protest, Penelope continued to rage. "I would never have believed that *you* would stoop to such a dastardly trick!"

"I would not!" Corbett protested his innocence as Penelope strode toward the door.

"Well, thank goodness no one knows we are here together, so it is your word against mine," she turned and informed him coldly. "And if you try to bruit this tale about, thinking to shame me into marriage, I shall call you a wretched liar to your face and . . . and I shall have my cousin Bradley call you out to defend my honor."

My gracious! she thought, surprised at her own fury. She *was* angry if she could make that kind of threat.

"So there! I shan't marry you, Corbett Remington. Not now, not ever!"

With her hand on the doorknob, she looked back to him. "And I shan't let you maneuver me into a situation like this ever again! Thank you very much, Corbett. I have learned far more than just dancing tonight."

CHAPTER
TWELVE

Lord Bellingsford had planned something a bit different to entertain his guests this morning. The majority of the house guests leaped into this activity with as much zeal as they did everything else, although several decided to remain indoors, playing at cards. Penelope complied with his wishes, albeit without much enthusiasm. Mrs. Dilley had not been so fortunate.

"I truly am not dressed for such rusticity," Mrs. Dilley complained as she was lifted into the large hay wagon. Panting heavily and fanning herself vigorously, she settled down beside Margaret. She sputtered at the rising chaff and picked at bits of straw which stuck to her gown.

Slowly, the oxen began to pull the lumbering wagon across the field toward the home farm.

Mrs. Dilley jabbed her daughter in the ribs with the sticks of her fan. When Margaret turned a startled gaze to her mother, Mrs. Dilley said sternly, "I want you to know that I am accompanying you on this miserable outing today specifically to make certain you do not ignore Mr. Remington. However do you expect the man to make you an offer when you speak to every other gentleman here, yet you act as if Mr. Remington were not even in the same room as you?"

"You look rather green, Mama," Margaret observed without much interest. "If you do not mind my saying so, 'twas probably ill-advised for you to come today at all." Margaret then turned to look at the marvelous vista of Bellford Manor that a gap in the foliage afforded.

As everyone alighted in the paddock of the home farm, Lord Bellingsford began to lead them immediately toward the large barn.

"Do watch your step," his lordship warned as the gentlemen assisted the ladies to make their way through the tall grass and over the uneven terrain in the enclosure.

Mrs. Dilley had apparently recovered from the indisposition caused by the bumpy wagon ride. She quickly seized Margaret's arm and propelled her in Corbett's direction. He bowed politely and offered her his arm.

"Come with me, little cousin," Bradley invited.

He had wasted no time in coming to her side, Penelope observed with dismay. Small wonder. She had barely talked to Corbett, nor he with her, all morning. Without his forbidding presence, she was easy prey for Bradley.

"I would not want you to trip and fall," he said, gingerly taking her by the elbow as she crossed the field. "You might be injured."

"I shall not trip," she told him firmly. She withdrew her arm from his grasp. "This may surprise you, Bradley, but, unlike most of the ladies here, I have had a great deal of practice walking across fields."

Bradley laughed. "So you have. I would wager a lady with your poise and agility would be graceful anywhere you trod."

Penelope decided that pretending an intense interest in watching birds in flight overhead was an excellent means to void retching because of Bradley's extraordinarily fawning sentiment.

"I want you all to see the marvelous new bull I purchased," Lord Bellingsford announced excitedly.

"Bull!" Mrs. Dilley exclaimed. "The only beef I care to see should be served on a silver platter upon my dining room table, not upon the hoof!"

"Oh, join us, Mama," Margaret called back to her. "Do remember why you are here today." She fairly dragged a cautious Corbett along with her as she strode enthusiastically across the field.

Penelope, following behind, shook her head with disbelief. No one in their right mind dared stride a cow pasture without more care as to the placement of their steps. Still, she thought as she looked on with amusement, if anyone could march the cow pasture unscathed, 'twould be Margaret.

"Oh, dear!" Mrs. Dilley cried in dismay. "I do not believe what I have just trod upon!"

Mrs. Dilley was solicitously escorted back to the wagon. While a maid cleaned her shoes, she settled herself into one of the chairs brought along for the al fresco luncheon under the elms that was scheduled for later. She refused to be moved until then.

For a while, Penelope watched with interest the enormous new bull and the rest of the animals. Still, she found little fascination with things that she had grown up watching.

The largest billy goat apparently decided that one of the ladies' reticules looked extraordinarily tasty. While Bradley and several other gentlemen chased the hungry offender away, Penelope managed to escape Bradley's constant presence, and slip away from the rest of the group.

Once again Penelope could enjoy the sheer simplicity of a solitary walk through the soft grass of the broad stretch of pasture. The mottled expanses of green and brown were a welcomed contrast to the rich tapestries and lush velvets with which she had been surrounded for over two weeks. She had not realized how truly homesick she was until now.

She stopped to lean against a low stone wall that separated this pasture from a fallow field. Beyond lay a small woods, the leaves stained yellow and orange by an early frost.

"Are you tired?" Lord Ormsley asked, rousing Penelope from her introspection.

"Oh, no, my lord," she answered. "I am glad I came. The farm is very beautiful this time of year."

"Indeed. I wish my own farms looked as well," he said ·

wistfully. "Of course, I have been told that Remington Court was once every bit as prosperous and grand," he stated proudly. "Did you know that it began as a Saxon fortress?"

"No, I did not," she replied. "How very interesting to live somewhere so old."

"I should like you to see it someday when—" His lordship hesitated. "Some other day," he finished. "Any building requires care, but when an edifice is that old, it requires constant maintenance. Did you know my family was titled when the Bellingsfords were still polishing someone else's swords," he told her with a little chuckle.

Penelope could see the proud gleam that brought renewed youth to Lord Ormsley's deep blue eyes.

"Of course, remember, young lady, mere pedigree is nothing with which to be impressed," he told her, sternly shaking his finger toward her to better emphasize his point. "The worthwhile accomplishments of the family are. It breaks my heart to think that I have been unable to do my part to improve Remington Court."

Lord Ormsley's voice had dropped low. It seemed to Penelope as if he was no longer aware of her presence, but was mulling over his own problems aloud. She was embarrassed by being made privy to his innermost thoughts, yet she did not know how to extricate herself without appearing inordinately rude.

"Wheat prices and the weather have been so erratic lately that it is difficult to plan for anything from one season to the next. I wanted to have the roof of the East Wing, which was badly damaged by the last winter's snows, repaired. However, Corbett convinced me to invest in livestock instead." Suddenly his lordship turned to Penelope and demanded, "I do not suppose you have read any of the latest pamphlets on the selective breeding of beef and dairy cattle?"

"Not recently," she replied.

He grinned at her. "I have not either, but Corbett is keen on them. He maintains if we improve each breed of domestic animal to its optimum productivity, we would not only increase the prosperity of every farmer, but would make milk and other healthful foodstuffs available to even the poorest people and their children, making them more energetic workers."

Penelope listened with increasing interest. She had believed Corbett cared only for what diversions he might find in London. She had no idea Corbett was interested in the welfare of livestock and indigent children.

"Corbett has even been conducting experiments in the hope of improving our herds of cattle," Lord Ormsley told her. In his voice, she could not miss the tones of a proud father.

"I had no idea Mr. Remington was a man of such varied talents," Penelope remarked.

Lord Ormsley chuckled. "Of course, the boy is correct. With our estates productive once again, I could make whatever repairs or additions I wished."

He kicked at several clumps of grass as they continued to walk along. "We could have done both if poor old Cousin Edmund had not lost everything when the treasurer of the Brinhampton Canal Ltd. absconded with all their funds and the firm was forced to declare bankruptcy."

Lord Ormsley looked up at Penelope, his blue eyes wide with a mixture of embarrassment and chagrin. "Oh dear," he said. "I forgot. That is a deep, dark family secret. I can trust you to keep a confidence, can't I, m'dear?"

Penelope nodded reassuringly. "Certainly, my lord. I shan't tell a soul."

"I mean about poor old Cousin Edmund," he clarified. "Not about Corbett's interest in agriculture and animal husbandry."

"Oh, about both, if you wish, my lord," Penelope said. "I . . . I had no idea Corbett was so interested in his family's estates . . . in that fashion."

Indeed, Penelope *was* greatly surprised. She had supposed the estate his father had inherited to be quite productive. She had never imagined that he might need a fortune, not to settle gaming debts and to pay off the bills for jewelry for various mistresses, but to set to rights wrongs done to the previous lord by unscrupulous investors. He needed the money to repair a home that both he and his father loved.

Penelope felt the sharp pangs of conscience. 'How wrong I have been!' she thought. 'If only I could admit my error and apologize to him.'

'Too late now,' she answered herself. All her old doubts began to assert themselves again. 'After all you have said and done, he will never listen to you now. At any rate, would you want him? Regardless of what noble aspirations prompted his actions, that is still no reason to use you so poorly.'

Penelope felt her heart grow colder as she was forced to agree with the more logical inner voice.

Penelope lay in her bed that night, sleepless once again. She still could not believe what she had witnessed. Before the evening's entertainment commenced, Mr. and Mrs. Dilley and Lord Ormsley had stood together and called for the attention of the assembled guests. Joyfully, they had announced the betrothal of their daughter Margaret and son Corbett.

Margaret and Corbett had been standing at opposite ends of the salon, but the crowd of well-wishers had drawn them together and pushed them to the fore, along with their parents. They had seemed bemused by all the congratulatory handshakes and embraces, but had smiled their polite acceptance nonetheless.

Penelope had been so upset she could barely see straight. Her blood had roared in her ears so loudly that she had barely heard the conversations going on about her the remainder of the evening.

'Oh, the devil take that wretched Corbett Remington!' she raged as she sat bolt upright in bed and stared out into the darkness. 'The man has been nothing but trouble to me from the first day I laid eyes on him!'

She rose from the bed and donned her dressing gown. Softly, she padded back and forth over the carpet. She was averse to considering the import of what had happened, yet incapable of thinking of any other matter. Completely miserable, she pulled off her dressing gown and threw herself back upon the bed, to continue to toss and turn.

Whatever else she had thought of Corbett, surely she had never imagined him to be quite so coldhearted and calculating. How sad to discover that she was wrong.

When she had refused him, he certainly had wasted no time in becoming betrothed to another heiress, had he? 'Twas not so much that he was marrying the hapless Margaret for her fortune—'twas the sad fact that, after four years, he was finally marrying someone else. She could not bear to think of him marrying anyone but her. It hurt her even to imagine him holding someone else close to his firm body, to imagine his warm lips kissing someone else, imagine them lying together in bed.

"Penelope, are you awake?" came the familiar cry through the darkness.

If she had not been, Penelope believed that voice would have surely wakened her. As a matter of fact, there had been moments when she believed Margaret could waken old Squire Wilkins, six feet under.

"Yes, come in," Penelope answered.

Penelope heard Margaret stumble into her bedchamber and slam the door tightly shut behind her. She could hear her colliding with the furniture, and loudly telling the offending furniture precisely what she thought of it, as she made her way across the bedchamber in the darkness. Suddenly the bed curtains were pulled back to reveal Margaret, wearing her night rail and dressing gown, with a very worried frown on her face.

Was Margaret out of sorts with her? she wondered. Penelope reflected that she had often been a fool, but she had never been deliberately rude.

"Have I offered you my very best wishes on your forth-coming marriage, Margaret?" she asked.

"Indeed. Several times."

'Oh, dear,' Penelope thought. 'I *was* befuddled if I do not remember wishing her well not once, but several times.'

"Well, then surely you should have double the happiness," Penelope said brightly, trying to hide her own errors.

"And won't I just be needing it, too?" Margaret asked glumly as she slumped down onto the edge of Penelope's bed.

"Margaret!" Penelope exclaimed with surprise. "I . . . I thought you would be happy. You . . . you *seemed* happy when they made the announcement."

"What else was I to do if I did not want to appear a fool in front of all those people? *I* knew nothing of that blasted announcement until they made it!" she wailed.

"How could they do that to you?" Penelope asked. "This is not the dark ages, nor some heathen country, where a lady may not choose her own husband."

"The other night, Mama and Papa and Lord Ormsley took me off to the side and asked me if I wanted to be a viscount-ess," she explained. "Well, of course I did! Wouldn't you?"

Penelope did not really give a fig for titles. She had wanted Corbett long before the issue of his prospective title ever reared its ugly head between them.

"The next thing I knew, I was betrothed to Corbett Remington, of all people," Margaret complained. She crossed her soft white arms over her plump breasts and pouted. "I do not want to marry Corbett Remington."

"You do not like Corbett?" Penelope asked incredulously.

"Oh, he is nice enough, I suppose," Margaret replied with a noncommittal shrug.

'Nice enough!' Penelope silently repeated. 'Corbett is wonderful and handsome and witty. I had considered Marga-ret so intelligent. How could she adjudge Corbett as merely *nice enough*?'

"With Papa's income, I have been besieged by fortune

hunters—despicable characters, each and every one—ever since I made my come-out," Margaret explained.

"Then why are you marrying Corbett? Do you not consider *him* a fortune hunter as well?"

"Well, in a way, yes," Margaret conceded. She heaved a heavy sigh. "But a girl in my position can hardly avoid them, can she?" She looked up at Penelope. "Do not worry," she warned. "You will discover what I say is true once you have made your come-out this spring."

Penelope wisely refrained from observing that one need not go to London to be bothered with fortune hunters.

"So, I suppose I could do worse for a husband," Margaret continued. "After all, he *is* one of the most handsome fortune hunters I have ever encountered."

Penelope again felt the pricks of jealousy when she heard Margaret discussing Corbett in such favorable terms.

"He is a quiet fellow, so I suppose I shall still be able to do exactly as I please without him making too much of a fuss," Margaret continued to consider her future as a wife.

Penelope could not help but recall Corbett's reaction to her when *she* tried to do exactly as she pleased. 'I suppose one is always a bit more tolerant of the people of whom one is especially fond,' she thought sadly.

"But Corbett is such a dry old stick," Margaret was complaining again. "He is no fun at all, Penelope. Truly!"

Penelope wondered if she and Margaret were discussing the same Corbett.

"He's not like Lord Ormsley at all, you know." Margaret looked extremely blue-deviled. "'Tis difficult to believe they are kin."

She lifted her head to glance about at the bedcurtains, then dropped her gaze to study her hands as she twisted the end of her night rail into a long, thin rag.

"When they asked me if I wanted to be a viscountess, I didn't think they were talking about sometime in the future," Margaret explained. "I thought they meant now. Oh, Penelope, I want to be a viscountess *now*."

Penelope cautiously regarded Margaret as the girl sat fidgeting at the side of her bed. She did not need any special prescience to see in what direction Margaret's conversation was headed. A tiny bit of hope peeked through the dark clouds of despair which had enveloped her.

"Well, in order to do that, you will have to find an unmarried viscount, won't you?" Penelope asked.

"I *have*," Margaret stated earnestly. She hung her head and twisted her fingers in her lap. Perhaps for the first time in her life, Margaret said quietly, "Now if I could only convince *him* of it."

Penelope would have wagered next quarter's allowance that Margaret would have an easier time of convincing Lord Ormsley than Penelope would ever have of convincing Corbett.

'I was not very kind the last time I spoke to him,' she admitted to herself as she sat alone in her bedchamber after Margaret had departed. 'Will he ever be willing to listen to me again? Well, at least I did not give in to that urge to kick him!' she reassured herself. 'Perhaps he will take that into consideration when I offer my apology.'

She wanted to talk to Corbett again. But how could she tell him that she had reconsidered? The very possibility of him marrying anyone else had shown her the truth of how much she still loved him, how much she still wanted him.

It did not matter to her that he married her only for her fortune. She only knew that she loved him. Four years had been too long to be separated from him. She could not face the long years ahead without Corbett. How could she tell him she would marry him—if only he would still have her?

Lord Ormsley paced the library, back and forth across the deep carpet. His gray brows were drawn into a deep frown that made so many wrinkles across his forehead that they fairly reached to the top of his balding head. Suddenly he drew to a halt in front of Corbett.

"No! I shall *not* dismiss the matter without a good reason.

And I most assuredly will not allow you to cry off this betrothal. Why *don't* you want to marry the girl?" Lord Ormsley demanded angrily.

Corbett pressed his lips together tightly. If anyone else had done this to him, Corbett would have laid the fellow out. But this was his father whom he loved and respected. He had thought his father loved him. Then why had the man tried to ruin the rest of his life without consulting him first?

Corbett tried his best to contain his own anger and frustration. He answered evenly, "Because you and the Dilley's and that hoyden—"

"Mind your words, son," Lord Ormsley cautioned, wagging a thick finger under Corbett's nose. "Miss Dilley is a fine girl, and I shan't have you—"

"But she consented to this fiasco as well," Corbett protested.

"She knew no more of it than you did," Lord Ormsley admitted.

Corbett's frown began to lighten at this news. "So you and the Dilleys arranged the betrothal without the knowledge or consent of either myself or Miss Dilley?"

"What do you mean, without your knowledge? I know you're not blind nor stupid. Could you not see why we have been throwing you two young people together so often—well, we've been *trying* to," Lord Ormsley grumbled. "You seem more interested in Bellingsford's milk-and-water daughter. Oh, not that she ain't a sweet little thing, and well-spoken, too, for all her humble upbringing, but . . . well, I just felt that Miss Dilley suited you better."

"But this is not the dark ages, nor some heathen country." Corbett tried to couch his protest in the most rational of terms—although at the moment, he felt anything but rational. "Can a man not choose his own bride?"

At this, Lord Ormsley began to pace once again. "But you did *not* choose! I have been waiting four years for you to marry and beget me a grandchild and you have not done your duty—by me or the estate. Therefore, I *had* to take matters into my own hands."

Corbett made no reply.

"I did it for you, boy," Lord Ormsley told him earnestly. He placed his hand on Corbett's shoulder. "Why else do you think I have been putting up with the antics of that horrid old cat, Mrs. Dilley? 'Twas for your sake! Yours, and our posterity."

Corbett tried to remain calm as he asked, "Father, did you never stop to think that I did not love Miss Dilley?"

"Love? Balderdash!" His lordship threw up his hands in despair. "What does love have to do with marriage? Do you think I loved your mother when I married her?" he demanded.

"Well, yes," Corbett stated quite frankly. "I rather thought you did."

Lord Ormsley drew in a deep breath. Then he was silent for a long while. At length, he lifted his blue eyes to his son's.

"Well, yes, Corbett," he admitted quietly. "You know, actually, I did."

Lord Ormsley settled back into a deeply upholstered chair. His eyes took on a contemplative haze.

"I loved her as soon as I saw her, sitting atop that little bay mare of hers, riding over the heath—couldn't ride for beans, she couldn't. But she sang like an angel. I knew I couldn't live without her as soon as I laid eyes on her. That is why I married so young when all my friends were still sowing their wild oats."

Lord Ormsley looked up at Corbett. "And you know, boy, I loved her more and more as the years passed—even after she was taken from me so suddenly and much too soon. I never was the same after your mother died," he said, shaking his head sadly. "I was happier the few years I was married to her than I had ever been in my entire life."

Lord Ormsley suddenly sat bolt upright in the chair and glared at Corbett. "That is why I want to see you married and happy, my boy. And Margaret is just the one to do it," he insisted. "Why, she's a capital girl! Splendid dancer, although she is not much of a rider. Hearty appetite for such a little lass. Sings like a veritable angel. Not so hard to look upon either. Any man in his right mind would jump at the chance to marry a wonderful girl like her! Makes a man feel good just being around her. Why, I have not felt like this since before your mother died—Oh, merciful heavens! The devil take me!" he cried, springing up from his chair. "What a fool I have been not to have seen!"

Lord Ormsley's voice trailed away and his eyes took on a different type of gleam—one that Corbett never expected to see in his father's eye, especially not at *his* age. His lordship rushed from the room without so much as a good-day to his son.

Corbett smiled. He did not mind his father's abrupt departure in the least.

CHAPTER
THIRTEEN

"CORBETT WAS QUITE correct, my dear Ermentrude," Lord Bellingsford told her. "In a gown of white, you do look a veritable angel."

Penelope smiled. Oh, why did his lordship have to bring up Corbett Remington at a time like this?

She took a deep breath and pressed Lord Bellingsford's arm for reassurance before she descended the long flight of stairs into the ballroom. She was astonished at the change that she saw below.

A thousand tapers, affixed in two, huge brilliant lusters, now shed their light upon the golden scene. Cheery fires blazed in the twin marble hearths at either end of the ballroom. Hidden high up in the musician's gallery, a small orchestra played. Spectacularly attired guests thronged the dance floor.

The ballroom had been dark, silent, bleak, and cold when she had left it on the night Corbett, in the guise of a dancing lesson, had tried to entrap her into marrying him. How different it looked now! And yet Penelope felt as if nothing that truly mattered to her had actually changed.

At the ball Lord Bellingsford had held only a few weeks previously, Penelope had merely been an impoverished scullery maid, with no hope of marrying the one man she had ever loved. Now, she was a lady, adorned with silk and pearls, yet all this had not made one bit of difference. She still had no hope of ever marrying the man she loved.

The ball was very much as she had envisioned it. She had

indeed allowed a properly chastened Gwenyth to fasten the ribbons of her slippers, as well as attend to other important tasks, while Margaret had solicitously overseen the entire process of Penelope's adornment.

Penelope knew she looked extremely elegant attired in the white silk ball gown Mme. Dupres had recently completed. She smiled when she recalled how Margaret had complained that the gown was not as stylish nor as well-made as something Penelope might have been able to purchase in London—but in the country, Margaret assured her, one need not adhere quite so slavishly to the dictates of fashion. At any rate, it did not matter what one wore, her friend told her, when one was as lovely as Penelope.

Penelope acknowledged that she did feel extraordinarily beautiful as every young gentleman there gazed enraptured while she descended the staircase. Everything was as lovely and exciting as she had ever imagined it could be—except that it was not Corbett Remington who offered his hand when she reached the foot of the stairs.

"How lovely you look this evening, little cousin," Bradley said as she took his hand. "And I am the lucky man with the great good fortune of claiming this dance."

The young gentlemen who clamored about her released, in unison, a sigh of despair.

"Have no fear, gentlemen," Penelope quickly reassured them all. "I have no intention of allowing my cousin to claim *all* my dances this evening."

The young gentlemen released, in unison, a sigh of relief, while it was Bradley's turn to look sullen.

"I am very pleased that you would allow me even just this one dance with you," Bradley said as he escorted her to the dance floor.

He held his gloved hand out for her to place hers in his, then rested his other hand against the center of her back. His touch was so light that she barely felt it. He maintained a properly discreet distance between them.

Although she had rejected him, Bradley had still not resumed his excessive drinking, Penelope noted with satisfaction. His eyes were clear, his breath fresh. Perhaps the experience had had some sort of redeeming effects on Bradley after all. Perhaps there was hope for him yet.

"Bradley, just because I will not marry you does not mean that I would not at least dance with you," she told him. She even felt comfortable enough to spare him a friendly little grin.

While the corners of Bradley's mouth turned up in a melancholy smile, his eyebrows drooped over his sad amber eyes. "My dear little cousin, 'tis true, your refusal—not once, but twice—of my very honorable proposal of marriage cut me to the quick. Still and all," he commented with a great sigh, "life does go on. I suppose I must learn to live with my disappointment. Perhaps after all, if I cannot have your love, I will value your friendship. May we still be friends, Penelope?" he asked tentatively.

'Twas bad enough to be related by blood to Bradley. She would never have willingly chosen him as a friend. But, as they had been thrown together by fate and bound by kinship, and as she had been fortunate enough to escape marriage to him, Penelope supposed she could be magnanimous now.

"To own the truth, I am rather proud of you, Bradley," she told him. "You are taking your disappointment so well. That is very sensible of you."

"Sensible? Yes, I am very sensible, if nothing else," he said. His lips pressed tightly together as if that were the only means he had of keeping himself sensible.

Suddenly he swirled her about to a grand crescendo of the lilting strains of music. Penelope had to concentrate very hard upon her steps so that she did not trip over Bradley's feet. Surprisingly enough, she managed to make contact only with the smoothly polished floor.

"You dance divinely, dear Penelope," Bradley said, reverting to a more sedate style of movement. "Wherever did you learn to waltz so well?"

'Wherever indeed,' Penelope recalled wistfully. As she

had made Corbett swear never to tell, she felt she could do no less. Therefore, she merely commented, "You too dance very well, Bradley."

"'Tis no doubt a family trait."

"No doubt," she replied without enthusiasm for any family trait that connected her to Bradley.

Penelope had thought Bradley to be the most obsequious flatterer she had ever encountered, yet by the time she had danced with a mere four or five different partners, she felt she could say the same for every young gentleman in the room. In no time at all, she found herself heartily bored with their insincere—and even with some of their sincere—flatteries.

How she wished that it was Corbett with whom she were dancing! Even if he did not flatter her, she missed the way they bantered and bandied their little quips between them.

She continued to dance and converse politely with each new partner. But although she continually searched for him among the throng, Corbett was nowhere to be seen.

'I suppose he is here somewhere . . . with Margaret,' Penelope thought sadly.

If he were with Margaret, apparently the unfortunate girl had been unable to confront her parents with the unsuitability of her match with Corbett, or she had been unable to convince Lord Ormsley of the definite desirability of another, more likely match.

'Poor Margaret,' she thought sympathetically. Then, when she recalled that her friend's freedom was incontrovertibly linked to hers, Penelope added, just a bit selfishly, 'And poor me.'

Even if he were free, Corbett would never return her love. Not even her fortune would be enough to induce him to marry her now.

How could she ever find happiness on her own without Corbett? She would never marry, inevitably Bradley would, she supposed. As the future Lord Bellingsford, someday he must. Perhaps Penelope could let a cottage somewhere nearby, visit him and his family for Christmas dinner, be a doting, eccentric old "auntie" to his children.

'I suppose, for the rest of my life,' she thought, feeling exceptionally sorry for herself, 'I shall just have to be content with what joys other people will allow me to share.'

When Penelope could finally take a moment's respite from the mad whirl of the dance, she noted that Margaret was every bit as busy as she, frolicking from one partner to another—and, to Penelope's knowledge, not a one of them had been Corbett Remington.

'But if he is not with Margaret, where is he?' Penelope silently cried. She felt a momentary surge of panic when she thought he might have left Bellford Manor entirely.

Her heart contracted with the dreadful thought that, if he had indeed gone, she might never see him again. She might never again have the opportunity to tell him that she loved him and wanted to be with him, even if he loved her only for her fortune, and not for herself.

Penelope looked up to see Lord Ormsley making his way across the dance floor. Her face brightened with a smile. 'Twas no guarantee, she knew, but if his lordship was here, perhaps Corbett remained as well. Perhaps there was still a chance—if only she could find Corbett, talk to him . . .

Hoping that his lordship might lead her to Corbett's location, she watched him. But Lord Ormsley stopped outside the circle that had congregated about Margaret.

"Come now, all you young bucks had best step aside," Lord Ormsley declared as he boldly broke through the crowd. "You've had your chance. 'Tis high time age and wisdom supplant mere youth and enthusiasm."

"'Tis not fair, m'lord! You must give us a chance," the young men protested.

"Now, now," Margaret said, smiling sweetly into each and every adoring young face that surrounded her. She rose and moved to Lord Ormsley's side. "You would not want his lordship to think me ungrateful for his kind attentions, would you?"

How strange to find herself in his arms now, Margaret mused as Lord Ormsley waltzed her about the large ballroom floor. Now, when she could finally admit to herself the feelings that she had tried, quite unsuccessfully, to suppress. Now she could admit that she was attracted to the man for another reason than the simple fact that he was fun to be with. The thinning hair above his forehead, the sprinkling of gray at the temples, the few little lines that crinkled at the corners of his deep blue eyes when he laughed, made him seem not older, but all the more endearing.

Lord Ormsley had stopped their swirl about the dance floor in front of one of the tall doors that opened out onto the terrace. Before the music had ended, he led her through the door and out into the darkness and privacy of the garden. He led her to a sheltered arbor and indicated a stone bench, just large enough for two to sit upon, *if* they sat very closely together.

She took a seat on her half of the bench.

"Miss Dilley . . . Margaret, if I may . . ."

How delightful to hear him say her given name aloud! "Oh, please do, my lord," she responded enthusiastically.

"I must talk to you quite seriously now, Margaret," he began as he settled himself beside her.

Although the bench was small, he sat so far away that their elbows barely touched. Margaret seethed inside with frustration. Oh, how unseemly 'twould be if she moved closer to him! So Margaret merely sat there, waiting.

"Margaret," he said at length. "I have made a grave error in betrothing you to my son. You see, he does not love you."

"Oh, I know that," she answered, dismissing his confession with a wave of her hand.

"You do?" he asked, quite surprised.

"Oh, yes. I have always known that Corbett was only marrying me for my fortune."

"And that does not bother you?"

"It did not—not in the beginning," she replied slowly.

"Then, may I ask, do . . . do you love him?"

"My parents have consented to this union, and I was under the impression *you* wanted it, so . . ." she said with a small shrug of her plump little shoulders.

"But do you love him?" Lord Ormsley insisted.

"Oh, he is a nice enough fellow," she conceded.

Lord Ormsley spun about in his seat to face her squarely. "But do you *love* him?" he demanded.

Margaret sat on the stone bench, completely silent, most probably for the first time in her life. At length, she said, "Please understand, my lord. Corbett is a very nice gentleman—and he is your son, and I would not want to say anything that you might misconstrue as an unfavorable opinion on my part regarding anyone dear to you. I would *never* wish to hurt your feelings. However, I think it probably best to own that I do not love him, if that is what you mean."

"I am rather glad to hear that, actually," Lord Ormsley said as he moved a fraction of an inch closer to her. "Because, you see, Corbett has informed me that he does not want you for his wife."

Margaret tried very hard not to show her immense joy and relief. Lord Ormsley might not be too pleased with a young lady who was happy to *not* be marrying his only son.

"Do you not want me as a daughter-in-law?" she asked, shyly turning her blue eyes up to him.

His lordship did not answer, as if he were not sure of how to continue. Margaret waited. She knew with absolute certainty what his lordship was going to say next. Oh, why would he not come right out and say it? Her patience was tried so severely that she thought she would grab him by the lapels of his coat and shake it out of him!

"I . . . well, quite frankly, no. No, I do not want you in my family as my daughter-in-law," he stammered. After several fitful starts, he drew in a deep breath, seized her hands in his, and finally declared, "Margaret, I want you for my wife."

Before she could reply—in the affirmative, most certainly—his lordship held up one hand as if to stop any remark she might make. "I know. I know. You probably think me a foolish, doddering old man with no better sense than to—"

"I do not!" Margaret declared, in tones so emphatic that no one could doubt her sincerity.

"You do not?"

In his surprise, Lord Ormsley almost drew his hands away from hers, but Margaret gripped them tightly so that he could not let her go. After all, she had no intention of letting *him* go!

"I have never thought you foolish or old or without sense, and I have *never* seen you dodder," she said. "As a matter of fact, I think you . . . you are . . . well, a great deal of fun to be with . . . and rather handsome, and . . . I love you, my lord."

"Peter," he corrected. "I would be pleased if you would call me—"

"Peter," she repeated his name, turning her smiling face up to him in the moonlight. "I would be delighted to be your wife."

At last Penelope espied Corbett! He was not possessed of inordinate height, or plumpness, or any other physical feature that might set him apart from the crowd. His hair was an unremarkable dark brown—not stark white nor flaming red nor anything else that would draw the eye immediately to him. Yet Penelope spotted him as soon as he entered the crowded ballroom.

She was so happy to see him at last that she wanted to run immediately into his arms. But he was still betrothed to another, as far as she knew. And all things considered, even if he were not, would he choose her now, regardless of the size of her fortune, especially after all the horrid things she had said to him?

Therefore, Penelope restrained herself. She forced herself to converse with people she had been introduced to, but whose names she could not have remembered if her life depended upon it! She allowed herself to be led about the dance floor by one tedious partner after the other. She even followed Lord Bellingsford's suggestion to take some refreshments in the dining room before she grew faint from lack of nourishment, although once there she found herself incapable of consuming more than a bite. Yet each time she was not otherwise engaged, Penelope watched Corbett as he strolled about the ballroom.

He was not with Margaret, she noted. As a matter of fact, Penelope had not seen Margaret for a long time. Most likely, she had just missed her in the dining room, where the girl was gathering more food to see her through another round of dancing.

If Corbett was not with Margaret, perhaps something had come of the girl's hopes after all. On the other hand, the two never had spent that much time together to begin with.

Suddenly, Penelope found herself confronted with Corbett. Her last partner had left her in her father's care, and Corbett had slowly, and very deliberately, made his way toward her from across the room.

He bowed low before her. "Is this dance not mine, Lady Ermentrude?" he asked.

Penelope made no pretense whatsoever of looking for any other partner. At this moment, there was no one else in the entire world with whom she wanted to dance. She wanted to smile at him. Oh, why was her mouth so dry and her lips so frozen that she could not smile, that she could barely speak at all?

"I believe it is," she managed to reply.

Corbett extended his hand to her. She placed her hand in his. She cursed the blasted gloves that she was forced to wear—no matter how fine they were—because they kept her fingertips separated from his warm touch.

He placed his other hand upon her back and drew her closer to him as he began to move her about the floor. Penelope smiled with the pleasure of being in his arms again. She wished the musicians could have continued playing this one single waltz for the rest of her life.

"I was not certain you would even speak with me," he said cautiously.

"I seem to recall four years passed when you did not speak with me," she reminded him with an admonishing grin. "I did not think a few days would make much difference to you."

His blue eyes held hers. "A few days can make all the difference in the world, Penelope."

"What difference has it made to you?" she summoned the courage to ask.

"It makes none to me," he said quite plainly. "I have not changed my mind regarding anything."

Penelope's pale green eyes grew wide. She believed her heart had ceased to beat within her breast. 'Twas only by swallowing very hard that she managed to make it start again. Nothing she had said or done had had any effect on Corbett whatsoever. He had not wanted her to begin with. Then he had only wanted her for her fortune, and now he did not want her at all.

She lowered her gaze to stare at the knot in his cravat. "It has made quite a big difference to me," she said slowly.

"How so?"

She had been afraid he was going to ask for clarification of her remark—and had been more afraid that he would not.

"I have had time to find out certain things . . . about myself . . . and about you," she said, looking pointedly up into his eyes. "I have had a little time to decide what is important to me and what is not."

"I already know what is important to me, Penelope," he said, drawing her closer to him with each step of the dance. "I have known for a long time. What have you decided is important to you?"

She was still trying to summon the courage to answer Corbett when Bradley approached them and tapped Corbett upon the shoulder.

"Can you not see this dance is claimed, Mr. Fairmount?" Corbett asked, frowning darkly.

"I have not come to claim the dance, Mr. Remington, but to claim my cousin," Bradley told him. Then, turning to Penelope, he asked quietly, "Might I have a word with you in private?" Looking about him to be certain that no one else had heard, he continued, "I think it best if the entire party does not know of this matter."

"What is it?" she asked.

"'Tis a private matter." Bradley glared haughtily at Corbett. "One that does not concern you, sir. I beg your indulgence." He bowed condescendingly low, dismissing Corbett from their company.

Patently ignoring Bradley, Corbett turned to Penelope and looked intently into her eyes. "I will do as *you* wish, my lady."

Penelope wanted Corbett to stay with her. However, not knowing precisely what Bradley meant to tell her, she decided that matters of a family nature were most probably best kept within the family after all.

"Please excuse me, Corbett," she said. Reluctantly, she disentangled herself from his embrace. "'Tis most probably some small matter quickly attended to."

Giving them both a backward glance, Corbett slowly moved away.

"Come, let us talk, Penelope," Bradley said. He gestured toward the staircase.

'Twas reasonable enough for Bradley to want privacy away from the noise and crush of the ballroom, she expected. But when he continued their walk toward the hallway, Penelope's heart leaped from her breast to throb at the base of her throat. If Bradley wished this much privacy to speak to her, there must be great trouble indeed.

Bradley looked very serious, and very worried, as he turned to Penelope. "I disliked interrupting your enjoyment, Penelope, especially of such a special night as this. However, there is a very serious matter that one of the footmen has just brought to my attention. I knew you would want to know."

"What is it, Bradley?" she asked, weary of his journey through the manor and now his long preface.

"I am sorry to be the bearer of sad tidings," he said. "One of the village boys was sent from the vicar. 'Tis Mr. Graves."

"Papa? What happened to him?" she demanded impatiently.

"It seems Mr. Graves had climbed up the church steeple to try to repair the belfry," he began to explain. He shook his head. "A man his age really should not be—"

"What happened to him!" Penelope cried, grasping at his coat sleeve.

"He fell and broke his back," he explained.

He placed his hand upon her shoulder in a gesture of consolation. Penelope did not feel consoled.

"I am afraid that Dr. Prescott does not hold out much hope for his survival beyond the morning. Mrs. Graves and the Reverend Mr. Wroxley are with him, but he mumbled something about wanting to see you one last time before he died."

"Then I must go to him!" Her mind flew through all the things she had to do. She began to pace the hall nervously, as if that would help to set her racing thoughts in order. "I must tell Father I am leaving. And I must get my cloak. Oh, 'twill take so long for the grooms to harness the horses," she lamented.

"I have already taken the liberty of sending a footman to order a carriage brought 'round," Bradley told her. "I sent your abigail to bring me your cloak, and I placed it in the carriage. I have also spoken to Uncle Roger. While he cannot leave his guests, he feels it best if you do go to Mr. Graves. I should be greatly honored to accompany you, Penelope, and offer whatever comfort I can."

"Oh, Bradley, you have thought of everything. This is so

kind of you." She placed her hand upon his. "You are turning into a true friend, aren't you?"

"Think nothing of it, Penelope," he said as he placed his arm about her shoulder and led her out the front door and down the steps toward the waiting carriage. "I am very happy to be doing this."

CHAPTER
FOURTEEN

PENELOPE HAD EXPECTED to see a great crowd thronging about the small cottage. Even if the people of the village had not been particularly kind to her parents in life, she knew the gruesome side of their natures would not allow them to miss the news of Mr. Graves' tragic death.

Even if he were already dead, she expected that her mother would at least have had a single candle burning. Instead, the cottage was completely dark and actually appeared to be deserted.

"Oh, no! Are we too late?" she said, her voice barely a whisper. As they drew nearer the darkened cottage, she clutched at the edge of the hood of the cabriolet until her knuckles were white.

"Is my Papa already . . . ?" She could not bring herself to say that last word. She could not even bear to think of it.

Jakes pulled the horse to a halt before the door.

If there had been people milling about, if the cottage had been lit—even with a single taper—Penelope would have jumped from the carriage and run the rest of the way to reach Mr. Graves all the more quickly. But the cottage was dark and she did not want to burst in upon the old man in the very throes of death. Worse yet, she did not want to confront the undertaker at his morbid task. Who in the parish, she wondered, would dig the grave for the sexton?

She waited for Bradley to assist her down, then approached the dark cottage slowly and silently, afraid of what she would find within.

Bradley pulled the weathered wooden door open for her, then bowed as he allowed her to enter first. Jakes stood to the side and held aloft the lantern that he had taken from the carriage. Still, the small lantern threw little light on the scene. The interior of the cottage remained in the shadows.

In a small, nervous voice, Penelope called, "Papa? Mama? Are you there?"

A muffled voice from within cried what sounded like "No, Penelope, no!"

Before she could turn to flee, Bradley had pushed her forcefully, propelling her into the cottage. She stumbled, but caught herself on the edge of the kitchen table, preventing her headlong tumble to the floor.

Bradley boldly strode in behind her. Jakes followed, slamming the door behind him. He set the lantern in the center of the table, then leaned his back against the door, thus blocking any means of escape.

By the light of the lantern, Penelope could finally see what had happened in the little cottage.

Mr. and Mrs. Graves sat tied to two small wooden chairs and to each other, with Mr. Graves' own stout ropes. Another empty chair was placed beside them.

Bradley gestured toward the chair. "I have been saving this place especially for you. Have a seat, my dear little cousin."

Penelope turned slowly toward him. She raised her chin and glared at him haughtily. She tried her best to keep her rage under control. If she fell into hysterics now, she would never be able to assess the situation.

"Bradley, if this is a joke, I fail to share your sense of humor. If this is not a joke, well then, this is the outside of enough!" she informed him indignantly. "How dare you endanger these innocent people! I demand that you release them immediately. Then you will take me home, after which, I expect you to give a full explanation—to my father—of your extraordinarily unusual behavior."

Bradley laughed at her. He pulled a pearl-handled pistol

from the inner pocket of his jacket, cocked it, and aimed it directly at her heart.

"Sit in the chair," he said.

"Well, whatever for?" she demanded of him, all the while remaining standing.

Actually, Bradley's actions were pitifully obvious. She knew he had wanted her fortune badly enough to marry for it. She was not surprised that he was desperate enough to kill for it, too.

If only she could delay Bradley long enough for some sort of rescue to arrive! She doubted that anyone would miss Bradley, but surely *someone*—Lord Bellingsford or Margaret or even Corbett—ought to notice that she was no longer at the ball. If only, when they did note her absence, they would be able to deduce that Bradley had taken her, and that he had taken her to the sexton's cottage.

If they did not . . . well, she could only hope that she would be able to think of a way on her own to extricate her parents and herself from this dreadful predicament.

She could hardly fight her way out, she reasoned. Not only were the men bigger than she, there were two of them. Her only recourse was to outwit them.

'Twould not be easy. Bradley was no fool. He had gotten her into this much trouble already. Still, he must have some weakness she could use against him. Penelope did not know Bradley very well—and no longer wanted to, either—but she knew enough of him to be certain that he would not be able to resist bragging to her of the clever scheme he had used to trap her.

"'Tis no sport when the prey is so easily caught," Bradley said with a deep sigh. Then he turned to Penelope with a sneering smile. "I knew you would never see through my plan, my ignorant country wench. Even now, I do not know if I should even bother to explain it. 'Twas too brilliant to be deciphered by the likes of you. Just look at how easily I duped you into coming here. You trusted me, you little fool. You actually believed I had changed!"

The man was not only devious, he was completely mad. She clenched her teeth, mentally berating herself for having allowed him to deceive her so well.

"I can understand your hating me, Bradley," Penelope said. She tried to speak to him as calmly and rationally as she could—which was extremely difficult considering the circumstances confronting her, and her own helpless rage. "But why should you wish to harm my parents? They have never done anything to you."

"Surely even *you* are not so obtuse that you cannot see to what end I have been working," Bradley said. "By tomorrow night, the news will be all over the county, and, doubtless, everyone will be *very* sad. Lady Ermentrude Fairmount, while paying a charitable visit to the impoverished family who raised her, was unfortunate enough to be caught in the ultimate prank—the cottage set afire by vandals, and the three hapless occupants trapped inside perished in the blaze."

"The authorities will see that this is no longer the work of naughty little schoolboys. They will find you out, Bradley, and catch you and punish you." Hoping that his overweening pride would keep him talking about himself and allow her more time to think, she asked, "How can you believe you will get away with this?"

"Because I have laid my plans very carefully," he answered, smug in his own conceit. He spoke to Penelope as if she were a very stupid child, capable of understanding only the simplest words. "For years, the village boys have played their pranks, but all they could think of was greasing ropes and loosening barrow wheels. 'Twas *I*, and I alone, who was astute enough to see a use for their childish schemes, designed as mere petty annoyances by incompetent, rustic minds. When I realized I would have difficulty in persuading you to marry me, I had another plan in reserve, using their tricks to obtain my own ends. I increased the intensity of the pranks, while still making it appear that any real damage was nothing more than an accident." He gestured to the elderly couple and the vacant chair. "All this will be seen as merely another prank that—dare I say it?—burned out of control."

"So it *was* you who burned our chicken coop! But why?" She understood it all now. Still, she had to ask. His explanation would take up precious time—time she desperately needed.

"You still do not see?" Bradley shook his head and clucked his tongue. "'Tis entirely your own fault, you know. If you had only been smart enough to fall in love with me, or even if you did not love me, to simply have married me. Then your fortune, which by all rights should have been *my* fortune, would have been mine anyway. Now, once you are dead, 'twill be mine by rights again."

"But you need not do this, Bradley," Penelope insisted. "Father is very generous. There is enough money for everyone."

"There is *never* enough money, my dear Penelope," Bradley stated coldly. "And that is why I must do what I must do. Please have a seat." He gestured to the empty chair.

"Bradley, 'tis *I* you hate. You need not harm my parents. Release them," she pleaded.

Bradley looked at her with feigned astonishment and asked, "But how else shall I be able to remove all suspicion from myself? Jakes will swear that he and I were in the stables, discussing my uncle's fine horses during the ball. And no one else will be the wiser."

"May you burn in hell for this, Bradley!" she said, her lip curling in disgust.

"I have no doubt that I shall, eventually," he said. He laughed and gave an insouciant shrug of his shoulders. "But while I am still upon this earth, I shall be having a ripping good time with Uncle Roger's money!"

Bradley handed his pistol to Jakes, who continued to train the muzzle upon her, and picked up a coil of rope that had been lying upon the table.

"Now, please have a seat, my dear," Bradley said as he

slowly approached her from across the room. He stood before her, so close that she could feel his breath upon her face.

She turned her head away from him.

Bradley seized her chin and forced her to look at him. " 'Twould have been so much more pleasant—for both of us—if you had only consented to marry me in the first place, my stubborn little cousin."

"I shall never marry you!" she hissed.

He jerked his hand away from her so quickly, the movement threw her head to the side. He glared at her. "I said have a seat, my dear. And I warn you, my patience wears extremely thin when I am forced to repeat myself too often."

When Penelope still refused to move, Bradley said, "Either you sit or Jakes will shoot you where you stand and set the cottage ablaze anyway, with the old people still inside—and still alive."

Penelope wanted to close her eyes to blot out the horrifying images that Bradley's words conjured in her mind. Yet she kept them open, afraid of what Bradley, or Jakes, might do if she did not keep a constant vigil.

"What a pity you could not fall in love with me," Bradley said, shaking his head. He smoothed his hand over her fair hair. "What a delight you might have been in my bed!"

His hand drifted down over her cheek to her throat. With his fingers to the side, and his thumb upon the little hollow at the base, he slowly began to close his hand until Penelope feared he would strangle her instead. She reached up and grasped his wrist with both hands, but no matter how deeply she pressed her nails into his flesh, he refused to release her. Just when she thought she would faint from lack of air, Bradley eased his tight hold.

"What a delight you might be to me yet," he said. His hand continued down her chest until it came to rest upon her breast. " 'Tis but a cottage, and a poor one at that, but it still contains a bed. And, you know, my dear, Jakes has done far more than many valets to assist me. I do believe I should offer him some sort of compensation, if he does not mind waiting his turn—"

Penelope slapped Bradley's face.

At this, Mr. Graves, still tightly bound and gagged, began shouting loudly and angrily, and jumping up and down as best he could, weighted down by Mrs. Graves and both chairs.

"So you do not like my plans for your daughter?" Bradley sneered. "Well, old man, what can you do about it now?" He turned back to Penelope. He hooked his finger in the top of her gown, and began to pull at the delicate fabric until it slowly began to tear.

Mr. Graves continued to stamp and shout until he succeeded in toppling Mrs. Graves and himself over onto the floor. Penelope screamed.

Suddenly the cottage door flew open. Corbett burst into the room.

Taken by surprise, Jakes did not even have the time to turn his pistol on the intruder before Corbett floored him with a crushing blow to the chin. The gun discharged harmlessly into the thatch above. Jakes, unconscious, fell against the kitchen table, upsetting it. The lantern crashed to the floor, igniting the small rag rug and the hearth broom.

Bradley lunged at Corbett, lashing him about the head with the loops of thick rope. Corbett backed up a pace or two, shielding his face with his upraised arms.

The fire crept up the curtains to the dry timber of the roof.

With a quick, deft movement, Corbett seized the rope and spun about, sending Bradley crashing backward into the wall. He wrenched the ropes from out of his hand.

Bradley's face was livid with uncontrolable fury. He lunged at Corbett, his bare hands poised to seize his throat. But his insane rage was no match for Corbett's strength. With two more swift strikes to the chin, Corbett knocked Bradley unconscious.

The fire raged up the walls of the cottage now, catching in the roof thatch.

"Run, Penelope, run!" Corbett cried, straining to make himself heard over the roar of the fire above them.

The burning thatch began to fall about them. Corbett seized Bradley's feet and began pulling him to safety through the door.

Corbett saw her still inside, hacking with Mrs. Graves' dull old kitchen knife at the ropes that still bound her parents.

"Penelope, get out of here!" he commanded more loudly.

"Blasted knife never did hold an edge!" Penelope muttered as she continued to chop at the thick rope. She spared only a moment to lift her head to protest, "I must release them!" she screamed. The noise of the fire was deafening now.

"I will get them! Save yourself!"

"You cannot do it all alone!" Penelope cried, all the while never ceasing her efforts to cut the tough rope.

With one last angry slash, Penelope severed the ropes that bound her parents. As Corbett dragged the still-unconscious Jakes to safety, Mr. Graves led his bewildered wife in a mad dash from the burning cottage.

"Where is Penelope?" Corbett demanded of them when he saw them come rushing from the burning building.

"I thought she was right behind us!" Mr. Graves cried, looking about frantically. He began to call, "Penelope! Penelope! Oh, no sir! You can't go back in there now."

The doorway was aflame, but Corbett could not hesitate even one second, or it might be too late. Heedless of Mr. Graves' protests, Corbett burst through the blazing doorway. He fought his way through the choking smoke into the cottage, all the while calling Penelope's name.

The smoke grew too dense. Corbett's mouth was hot and dry with the taste of the ash and smoke that filled the air. He dropped to his knees, where the air was suffocatingly hot, but still clear enough to see where he was going. Perhaps he could see Penelope's feet. He only prayed he would not find her unconscious—or worse yet, lifeless—body slumped on the floor.

The floor was littered with ash and bits of burning thatch. The walls were sheets of flame. Penelope was nowhere in sight.

"Corbett!"

He heard her coughing and calling to him through the haze that filled the room. Circling the tumbled heap of chairs and tangled ropes on his hands and knees, Corbett found Penelope standing in the small lean-to attached to the cottage.

The roof over the small addition had not yet begun to flame. The air was clearer in here. Corbett was able to rise.

She ran to him when she saw him. With immense relief, Corbett encircled her within his arms.

"Are you all right? What are you doing in here? Why did you not follow your parents? Why did you not get out when I first told you to!" he demanded. All the while he scolded, he could not help but run his hands over her head and face, her back and arms, making certain she had not been injured.

"The smoke . . . the falling thatch . . ." she said, still coughing to clear her lungs. "I could not follow . . . but there is a window . . . I could climb out." Suddenly she looked up at him and frowned. "I saw you escape. Why on earth did you come back into a burning building?" she demanded. "Are you insane?"

The timbers of the old cottage creaked and moaned under the strain as the fire spread.

Corbett gave her a gentle push toward the small window. "I suggest we discuss this outside. Immediately!"

Penelope stepped up onto her old bed. The feather mattress sagged and she struggled to keep her balance. She pulled herself up to the window.

"Begging your pardon, my lady. It cannot be helped," Corbett said as he placed both palms on her rounded derriere and lifted while giving a great push.

Penelope slipped through the window easily. She tumbled

to the ground, then turned to see Corbett's broad shoulders stuck in the small frame.

"Give me your hand!" she ordered.

Seizing both of his hands in hers, Penelope placed one foot against the cottage wall and began to pull him through while he pushed with his long, strong legs from the other side.

"I am stuck," he said. "I shall never get out."

"Push harder!" she ordered.

"Run, Penelope, before this whole building comes crashing down."

"I will not leave you. Now push!" she cried as she pulled with all her strength. Penelope heard her gown rip.

Corbett broke through the rotting wooden window frame and the crumbling brickwork. He stumbled to his feet and pulled Penelope clear just as the flaming roof crashed in behind them.

"My parents!" she cried.

Corbett followed her to the front of the cottage. He found her locked in her parents' arms as the three of them sadly watched their home go up in flames.

"Where is Bradley?" Corbett asked. He had no intention of allowing the blackguard to escape his much deserved punishment. "And that miserable valet of his? I shall catch them both," he vowed, "and make them pay for all the harm they have caused."

Mr. Graves, breathless, pointed in the direction of the woods. "The wretches regained consciousness, took one look at us and the burning cottage, and took off for the woods at a run," he explained. "I tried to catch them, but these old bones are no match for the speed of a coward."

The blaze drew a crowd of onlookers—villagers still clad in night rails and nightshirts, hastily pulling on shawls and buttoning breeches, as well as elegantly attired ladies and gentlemen, arriving from Bellford manor in their equally splendid carriage.

"How awful! How terrible!" they all voiced their sympathies. At last, the Reverend Mr. Wroxley made his way through the crowd.

"Please, take shelter in my home," he invited Mr. and Mrs. Graves. "Make use of the extra bedchamber until your house can be rebuilt."

"I shall have some food sent," Lord Bellingsford offered.

"I have some clothing," a well-dressed lady offered.

People were suddenly so much more kind. Still Penelope watched with relief as the crowd finally dispersed and returned to their homes.

"Will you be all right, m'lady?" the vicar inquired.

Penelope nodded.

"I have assured Lord Bellingsford that I shall see her safely home," Corbett answered.

Penelope watched as Mr. Graves led a bewildered, stumbling Mrs. Graves across the field toward the vicarage.

Penelope was left standing alone with Corbett. As the blazing cottage died down to embers, the night grew darker about her.

"Come, Penelope," Corbett said. "You cannot stay here all night. I told your father I would take you back to Bellford Manor."

"I suppose so," she answered, giving one last look to the ruined cottage that had once been her home. All trace of her former life was now gone. "Now I truly have nowhere else to go but to Bellford Manor."

Corbett placed his hand upon her shoulder and drew her to him. He felt woefully inadequate to the monumental task of consoling her.

Exhausted, she slumped against him for support. She coughed, ridding her lungs of the smoke and filling them with the fresh, cool night air. Her white silk gown was torn and singed. Her face was smudged and the soft tendrils of blond hair at the front were crimped from the heat. But, thank God, she was still alive!

He reached out and brushed the crinkled hair from her face.

"You are not only the most beautiful woman I have ever known," he murmured, more to himself than to her. "You are also the most courageous."

She opened her eyes and looked at him. "Thank you," was all she managed to say at first. Then she seemed to revive a little more. "How . . . did you know something was amiss?"

"It did not take too much intelligence to guess that Bradley was up to no good." He shrugged his shoulders. "On the other hand, perhaps I am just too suspicious."

Penelope looked away from Corbett to the glowing rubble that was all that remained of the cottage that had been her home for so long. "I am glad you are. He almost killed us," she murmured.

Corbett cradled her in his arms. He wiped a smudge of soot from her cheek.

"But how did you know where he had taken me?" she asked.

"I did not know, but Gwenyth did."

"Gwenyth?" she repeated incredulously.

"When I was searching for you, she told me that after Bradley had got your cloak, she watched him from your bed-chamber window, noting the direction in which he had taken you," Corbett explained. "From what she told me, there could be only one destination to which he would take you."

"Gwenyth, of all people," Penelope mused. "I must remember to thank her."

Penelope reached out her hand in the darkness and began to trace her fingers over the muscles and ridges of the strong knuckles in Corbett's hand.

"I . . . I must remember to thank you too, Corbett," she said softly. "I have no idea how I will ever repay you for all your kindnesses to me. . . ."

"Will you marry me?" he asked readily.

"But . . . but you are already betrothed to Margaret," she protested.

"Well, it seems that Margaret has decided to cry off our betrothal," Corbett told her.

He did not sound extraordinarily cut up over the matter, Penelope decided. "What a pity," she said. She did not think she hid her sarcasm very well. "You have been betrothed for so long." Still, she thought she at least ought to be polite. "But why should Margaret do such a thing?"

"It seems Margaret found someone else she would rather marry."

"Oh, I'm sure Mrs. Dilley has retired to her room with the megrims—or has caused Margaret to."

"On the contrary," Corbett said. "'Tis someone of whom her parents heartily approve."

Before she could stop herself, Penelope exclaimed, "But who could surpass you?"

"My father," Corbett answered.

Penelope's pale green eyes grew wide in the moonlight.

"Obviously, he no longer thinks of himself as too old for that sort of foolishness after all," Corbett explained. "And, apparently, Margaret never did."

Penelope chuckled. Corbett stood watching her intently for an interminable second.

Then, very slowly and very softly, Corbett asked, "Do you realize what this means to me, Penelope?"

But Penelope was laughing too hard to answer immediately.

"You think this laughable?" Corbett asked.

"Oh, no. Oh, I am so sorry, Corbett, if Margaret has hurt you. I know what it is to hurt, and I would never wish anyone to feel that way. Indeed, 'tis not laughable," she insisted, all the while still giggling. "But 'tis quite like Margaret."

"If the truth be told 'tis quite like my father, too." Corbett began to laugh with her.

He put his arm around her shoulders, then stepped just a fraction of an inch closer to her.

"But do you know what this means to *me*, Penelope?" he repeated his question.

Penelope stopped laughing. Suddenly, with Corbett standing so maddeningly close to her, the situation was not quite as funny as she had at first thought it. Corbett was now free to choose another wife.

She swallowed hard and managed to ask, "What will you do now, Corbett?"

"Now, I can marry anyone I wish," Corbett replied, smiling. "I have already asked you once, and you did not answer me. Penelope, will you marry me?"

"Why do you ask me now?" she whispered, unable to speak any louder because of the lump in her throat. "Your father has married his heiress. Your family's estates are saved. You no longer need my fortune."

"I need *you*, Penelope. I have needed you for as long as I have known you. The four years we were separated were hell for me. I could not bear to be without you—and I could not bear to be with you."

She pulled back from him slightly with surprise. He drew her close again.

"Every moment I am with you, I want you more than I can say," he explained. "But if I had married you then, I would have ruined my family—and if we had not married, I most probably would have ruined you. 'Twas for the best that I stayed away then."

"I thought you went away because you did not love me."

"I made certain you were released from prison. I taught you to waltz. I taught you to use the proper fork. I taught you what truffles are. I even risked my life for you! Does this not prove to you that you mean more to me than life—or money? If this does not show you the depth of my love better than any fading bouquet or badly written sonnet or off-key serenade, I am not sure what could!" he declared.

Corbett pulled her even closer to him so that she could feel his firm body pressing against her. She could feel his chest moving as his breathing became more erratic.

He slid his hands down behind her until he cupped his palms about the small of her back. He pulled her so close to him that there was no more room between them—not even for doubts. Penelope could feel his desire for her growing against her.

"I assume this means you truly love me," she whispered.

"Say you will have me, my love."

"Indeed, I shall," Penelope answered.

Then Corbett raised one hand to her chin and lifted her face to his. He kissed her, slowly and tenderly at first, just as he had that night in the darkened ballroom. Then his breath began to come in short gasps as his lips melded with hers.

"Of course, I can think of one very special way to show the depth of my love for you, Penelope. But, unfortunately, until we are wed, you will have to be content with mere bouquets and sonnets and kisses."

"Then, let us have a short betrothal," she suggested.

Corbett nodded his consent. "There remains one problem," he said. "How do you think you will like having Margaret for a mother-in-law?"